THE BOHEMIANS

BOOKS BY LAURIE BLAUNER

FICTION
The Bohemians
Infinite Kindness
Somebody

POETRY
Wrong
All This Could Be Yours
Facing the Facts
Children of Gravity
Self-Portrait with an Unwilling Landscape
Other Lives

THE BOHEMIANS

Laurie Blauner

Black Heron Press
Post Office Box 13396
Mill Creek, Washington 98082
www.blackheronpress.com

Cover art by Laurie Blauner.

The lines quoted on page 178 are from the poem "Ramona Speaks to the Rain" by Laurie Blauner, published in *Other Lives* (Owl Creek Press).

Thanks to Jerry Gold, editor and publisher. Thanks also to all my friends who are artists and writers, especially Rich Ives and Barbara Lindsay, for all their help, and to my husband, always.

"Life being what it is, one dreams of revenge."
—Paul Gaugin

"A harmoniously conducted picture consists of a series of pictures superimposed on one another, each new layer conferring greater reality on the dream."
—Charles Baudelaire

PART I

Underpainting

Leon discovered the newspaper article, nearly two years old, crumpled in the pocket of his jacket.

"Tiger Woman" Escapes
New York Post (Dec. 6, 1922)

"Tiger Woman" Clara Phillips, convicted of murdering her husband's lover, Alberta Meadows, an attractive 21 year old widow who worked in a bank, escaped from prison. Mrs. Phillips was dubbed "Tiger Woman" because a police detective said that when she employed a hammer claw on Meadows' face and body, Meadows looked like "she had been mauled by a tiger." After the deed Mrs. Phillips returned home in blood-stained clothes, threw her arms around Armour Phillips, her handsome oil-stock salesman husband, and reportedly said, "Darling, I have killed the one you loved most in this world. Now I'm going to cook you the best supper you ever had." Mrs. Phillips, a former hoofer, had only served a few days of her ten-year sentence before a hacksaw was smuggled into her cell. The fugitive swung to the roof of the prison on a rope and, barefoot. she boarded a waiting automobile driven by a man answering the description of her husband. The murderess is currently suspected to be in Mexico or Honduras.

What happened to her? She had been caught within a few months and was back in prison. And her husband? Had he married someone else? All those people with wonderfully sensational lives that Leon dutifully read about in the newspaper every morning. His own was as dull as dishwater. He tossed the article onto a nearby windowsill that was vibrating to the beat of the band's current song. Leon shook his blonde head just as a silver ashtray with a bird perched on its side flew past him, barely missing his neck. Someone screamed, "Watch out!" fashionably too late and then laughed in a caterwauling way. The ashtray skidded along the foyer floor, missing the feet of celebrating dancing girls, two graceless couples, and an energetic band full of musical hilarity. Leon tucked his hands into his empty pockets, looked around. He didn't know anyone. He wasn't sure why he had come all that way to the Beckers' party except that he didn't have anything else to do.

Lil, short for Lillian, surveyed the party in the large, iron-colored room, its grayness expanding and contracting like an old lung. Zinnias were fading, losing their petals, and thick, red, heavily scented roses took their places in the scattered vases that were gathered into the arms of maids. A woman in argyle stockings, red hair bobbed a bit too short, was having the jimjams in the corner of the Beckers' country house. Her skirt twitched at her knees, her hands were confused. A man approached her with a drink in his hand and said to her contorted face, "I see the enormity of my mistake."

He kissed her shaking hand and left, the Victrola singing behind her.

Lil's patron, Mr. Becker, was wearing a tuxedo like a circus ringmaster. Where was Mrs. Becker? Lil shifted horizontally, feeling muscles and hard bones beneath the thick skin below her, the body she was resting on. There was a deep, warm, animal smell, as if she were at the zoo. She closed her eyes and breathed, liking animals almost as much as she liked painting.

Lil swatted at some flies that worried the air just below the coiling smoke of her newly lit cigarette. he was still lying on her side. As she exhaled, her dress fringe shook. The sound was a lengthy sigh. The animal began to shift, but then didn't. Claws clicked on the wooden floor for a moment and settled. She thought about scratching her $1.25 silk stockings and then didn't. Lil was content. The flies, however, were still searching for something; unsure of the alternatives, they flew in complicated ellipses and ended up where they began. Stray light from the party highlighted the tiny clouds of their wings. They buzzed, but no more than some of the conversations Lil had overheard and immediately forgotten.

It was 1924 and Lil knew that there were so many ways to die accidentally. But none had struck her as vividly as the story about the woman who loved immersing herself in bathtub gin in her bathtub. Yet she managed to drown in it without tasting a drop.

She imagined the woman already drunk, climbing awkwardly into the bathtub, laughing, spilling her drink into the half-filled porcelain basin. She could have been talking to a man as she watched her fingers sway under the grainy, odorless liquid, her dress a weight as she sank into what she loved. Gin hugged her waist and shoulders. She rested her chin on the rim, wanting to drink it all down, a willing sacrifice. Her companion had probably already left. She was happy. Her arms were sinking stones. Then her eyes closed.

Lil found that dedication admirable. Art was being surrounded by what you wanted most without getting to enjoy it. Art was like that. Maybe it was human nature, trying to reach a sort of perfection that seemed impossible. The clear, overwhelming, burning liquidity of it went straight to her gut. She could drown in it. All of her men were like that gin too. She wanted who she wanted and yet she couldn't quite taste any of them.

Mrs. Becker appeared out of the crowd and, looking at Lil's reclining position, drunkenly said, "Comfort is relative. Sometimes you must offer up a Picasso sketch or raw meat. It simply depends upon the force of who is doing the asking." Funny for a patron to say, since she was one of the people doing the asking. The intentions were the same, mere noise.

Mrs. Becker disappeared again. The flies, though, wrestled continuously below Lil's shoulders like her thoughts.

She could feel a canopy of trees over the oddly shaped Victorian house, the gables cringing in the dark. The rambling porch was making a run for the fermenting, ruined-smelling lake. She had crushed too much late chickweed, walking yesterday while watching tiny, autumn insects swarming over its fusty, grieved, oily face. Even the balconies, meant to display the lovely profiles of lake, gardens, a gazebo, tennis courts, and carriage house, the one where the artists stayed, were all representative of an era that had vanished, one with porcelain in the bathrooms, silver platters with fruit, and crisp, white bed sheets. Just as all the house's features faded into the night, she missed New York City, which wasn't too far.

There were fifty-three ways Lil could position her cigarette holder. Many were mildly alluring for a twenty-six-year-old, some were deliciously obscene.She tried one.

She could feel coarse hair that wasn't her own bristling against her arm. A mouth moved, sighing, the lips pressing together again and again. Then it stopped. She watched the piano player, another sleepwalker, his dark, slick hair falling around his ears as his fingers tossed about the black and white keys. No one could hear him above the songs from the phonograph, although he appeared to be animated, enjoying his own music. She inhaled from the black, hard rubber of her cigarette holder; clouds filled her. Then they were outside her. She wondered if her body had changed the smoke somehow as it rose toward someone else's face.

She should have been composing a painting in her head. A group scene. Something Cubist, with its sense of isolation. Yet there was some connection to the world, through the outermost edges. The boundaries between objects and people seemed to dissolve. Blues and greens, white and black, a touch of red threaded through. Maybe later, when the partygoers had exhausted themselves with hooch. When they settled into their suits and dresses, then she could sketch them.

The moon peered through a window like another drunk-

en guest. The strange. pale curves and indentations reminded Lil of the white face of Leopold staring from the newspapers. Or was it Loeb? They had understood the randomness
of death without knowing its opposite, the disorder of creation.

   Lil's headband pinched behind her ears. She tugged it
slightly but allowed it to fall back because she liked the way
it looked. The yawn located below her rib cage stretched
out into sleep, in spite of the irritating cigarette smoke. Lil
noticed the man with hair the color of a lion's mane. He
wore a standard gabardine suit, wrong for this new time of
cars, smoking, drinking, and these parties. He was another
cog in the progress of machines and fashion, wide lapels,
a buttoned jacket, the matching brown little bungalow of a
hat split by a gray ribbon. If Lil's mother had been alive,
she would have found him lacking, would have asked her
daughter if she really was attracted to him.

   He stood back and touched inside his jacket, tapped his
crisp, white shirt as if he were checking on his heart. Or,
perhaps, it was just a nervous gesture; he didn't seem to
know anyone there except the Beckers. He removed his hat,
holding it like a plate. Lil hadn't seen him before. Partygoers usually breezed in and out of the Beckers' parties. He
had an angular face she would describe as "a biography of
longing"—but longing for what? Perhaps she would paint
it. Perhaps she would understand her own particular longing for men she couldn't have.

   There was a new vocabulary of seduction, and some
women used their eyes or their legs. Men misunderstood.
She hoped, as all women did, that the men would look

deeper, beyond the bones, skin, and hair, and the theatrically fringed dress.He watched her now, too, this man, as she moved the small hill of her hips, shadows scurrying across her as if disagreeing among themselves. She exhaled, blowing smoke toward the dark window with its skittering stars. She ran a hand through her orange fringe. She liked the rushed, obvious eye of the cigarette. Her gruff "sailor's" voice, as Marco called it, wanted to say something but she merely cleared her throat.

There was a warm body below her, its heat tucked against her side, the sparse, wooly fur. She petted a patch distractedly. Smoke from her holder reached for the moon and rose past it. It made it difficult to see the people moving about, hidden in swirls until they dissipated. Jazz blared from a Victrola. Automobile headlamps lit up the gables and shingles, the huge, old oak tree by the steps, a low window, an occasional tower, and weaving people as they noisily came and went. "Jiminy Cricket," a man yelled as he ran after a woman who jumped onto the running board of a car that was leaving. There was clanking and honking and the sounds of heavy machinery turning, and tires as they shifted and left their tracks. Some dancers tried the Charleston or the Black Bottom while the Beckers practiced a Turkey Trot in their formal, black and white clothes. The Beckers' heads faced toward Lil and then turned abruptly away. They were moving pictures to her. A game of Mah Jong clicked in a corner between songs. A woman in a cloche hat, with blue-lidded eyes, rose excitedly from her chair. She was chewing gum. A dark-haired man across from her wore a wildly red scarf at his neck as he concentrated on the colored tiles. Lil

thought this new time was oblivious to the former rituals
and unwritten laws for women, the prim gloves, the sen-
sible shoes, long skirts, a ban on smoking (except behind
closed doors), certainly no hint of sexuality. Surrealism jux-
taposed realities, the prim man in a chair looking out a window with a naked woman dancing around him. Everything
had changed. Subtlety was no longer necessary.

When Leon thought about death, which he rarely did, he
thought of machines losing their essential parts, not merely
a nail or a screw but something necessary like coils, motors,
transformers, condensers. So the machine was no longer
working. Or he thought of numbers being erased, forgotten. Only yesterday he sat down in a nickelodeon to see his
first motion picture show; shadows swarmed the screen,
images of Anthony and Cleopatra struggled into light and
dark. They beseeched, cried, raged, and flew across the flat
surface, resembling trapped birds, until the film jammed in
the gate arm and began burning. The smell was sharp, almost bitter. The screen became a black-edged ocean moving
backwards in time to its inception. Smoke billowed in small
waves.

"Fire!" someone yelled, and Leon heard wood splinter-
ing, felt the floor trembling as all the people ran out. He
was rushed along with the crowd, which quickly dispersed.
Outside an older man removed his glasses. Both lenses
cracked and fell from the frame into his open hand, burning
his fingers.

Mr. Becker's party made him think of the crossword-puzzle craze, better than the marathon-dancing and flagpole-sitting crazes still gaining popularity. That was how the Beckers had made the money that Leon watched for them. One thin crossword-puzzle book with its lines and squares made for a niece that had burgeoned into profitable themes, Biblical, Yiddish, and Women's among others. Now the books were even sent aboard steamers before they made their way across the ocean. Leon sometimes tried the puzzles, but they didn't seem to have a purpose. The words branched off from one another and didn't say anything.

A maid arranged oranges into a pyramid in front of a colored piano player. One rolled to the feet of a woman with dark circles below her eyes. Her foot kicked the orange beneath the piano. Music squeezed under the thick, orange skin. Shadows emerged in the shapes of bruises in the odd house. Leon breathed deeply, wiped his hands on his knees. The jazz sounded like a woman crying.

Leon sipped at his warm drink, felt his heart pulling his blood to the beat of the music. The Beckers swept across the floor, all black and white, their eyes fixed on each other. Leon thought of silence and absence as he stood before two paintings on the wall, one with strange clouds swirling in and out of trees, and the other with shivering birds recollecting warmth. "*The Haunting of Peregrines*," Mrs. Becker stated as she sailed by, her arms held aloft.

She turned and then Mr. Becker nodded above Leon's shoulder. "My favorite. Regrets depicted as clouds. *The Envoy of Sky*. Lovely, eh?"

"Yes," Leon said to Mr. Becker's face swimming back across the floor.

"The artist is here," his quick mouth said as the couple stopped for a moment. "You must meet her. There are all kinds of rumors about her, but we don't take stock in any of them. After all, she is an artist."

Someone brushed Leon's hair into his eyes from behind. The Beckers were gone. A song about dazed love played on the phonograph record. His drink wept onto his hand and he coughed nervously as the woman with dark circles under her eyes ran her pale fingers through his hair and then brushed it back. Leon had never been touched so casually. He wasn't sure whether he was annoyed or pleased. Leon heard too much sound, too much music, as arms reached high into the air and then fell, legs kicked up and receded. An ebb and flow all around him. The woman was small, thin, and full of fragile bones beneath a sequined dress that caught the light and threw it against his eyes. She bit her lower lip as she tilted her head and asked, "Well, do you want to dance or not?"

Leon wanted to tell her about Couéism, the adage that "every day in every way" we were all getting better. Or Buchmanism, how he began each morning with an hour of silence and how even at the college house parties, he had spent time alone with God. He knew about flappers, booze, urbanism, and mass consumption, about supply and demand. He knew what was going on, but he wasn't a part of what was around him. Maybe he needed to sacrifice more of himself. Instead he answered, "I'm sorry. I can't dance."

The woman snorted, lost her balance, steadied herself with a hand on his jacket. She left. He could still feel a slight warmth where the cloth had stopped her fingers, a damp spot, and the trailing odor of an archetypal, flowery perfume.

Leon went and stood by a window. His twenty-nine-year-old body seemed too large. That night the moon looked injured and hollowed out in parts. He had been in love once, but she had found someone else, had simply drifted away from him, and he hadn't called her to find out what had happened. His friends said he had "taken a shine to Mamie," but there was nothing sparkling about it. He had always felt nervous around her. He had wanted to remove his silly and offensive hands and offer them to her.

The stars at the window were fractured and drying into pieces like scabs. He stole a glance at a newspaper left open on a low table.

~

Wedding of "Mrs. Goodfellow" Never Takes Place

Miss Phyllis Reed, a reporter at the New York Times known as "Mrs. Goodfellow," a dispenser of free legal advice, was to be married to Felipe Carrillo, governor of Yucatan, Mexico two days ago. Yesterday Mr. Carrillo was shot to death along with several of his followers because of his upcoming reforms.

Miss Phyllis Reed met the Governor when she saved the life of a 17-year-old Mexican boy who was a convicted murderer on death row at San Quentin. She had taken a

special interest in Mexicans living in California who had
legal problems. She wrote about the boy in her columns
and because of his age there was an uproar that spared his
life.

~

Leon thought he wanted a heroine, a woman who could
leave a factory worker's life behind, who could dare to live
an extraordinary life. Someone who wasn't afraid to be
greedy. He hated the paltry way he coveted experiences,
hesitating this morning to even greet his secretary, the one
whose reddened lips he had thought about kissing. Alma
had suddenly cut her hair and had donned numerous bracelets that clacked as she took dictation, twisting his mind
elsewhere. "He's all wet," she'd say, scanning a newspaper,
and Leon didn't know who she was talking about. Yet a part
of him understood that he should be careful about whom he
admired because it could upend his life.

He plucked another drink from the silver tray held pen-
sively aloft and offered to him by a maid. He could see
where she had scratched her cheek, where three long lines
of red welts had risen as though three feathers were about
to sprout on her face. Leon thought of her as a bird perched
over the reflective surface of a lake, one that distorted his
own face as he lifted the last drink to his lips. He could see
that she resembled a heron, whose beak grew larger and
then smaller on the shiny tray. He wondered what she was
doing later. Should he have another drink?

He didn't know anyone here except the Beckers. There

were no children's toys to be repaired inside the house, no newfangled machines to discover and explore, no bills or payments to be made, and the only person he had met so far appeared not to have slept for days, wanted to dance, and was drunker than he was. He paused by the windowsill and a woman danced by so fast her nose was a smear. Half the room was singing the words to a song he didn't know, "Hello, my baby. Hello, my honey. Hello, my ragtime gal." Leon realized how nothing was his, not even his secretary. It took too many strange birds to make a woman. He imagined flying when he found himself in front of the Beckers' paintings again. He wondered what Miss Reed would do. He wondered how he could get another life.

Leon turned around and noticed the small woman lying across a lion rug whose mane was worn and shabby. Smoke coiled and hovered in the air above her headband and disappeared into the rafters of the Beckers' house. She tilted her head so her dark bob fell to one side as she looked him up and down with her one visible eye. The cigarette holder left her parted red lips slowly and more smoke escaped in widening circles. Smoke reached through her brow and then vanished. She threw her head back as if to laugh, but only stared at the ceiling and brought the holder to her lips again. Her face was a dark surprise. Orange fringe from her flapper dress hung like some exotic saddle across the back of the lion. He walked closer to her as all the small lives flitted around him, dancing, singing, drinking, talking, playing Mah Jong. His face opened toward her and he couldn't hear any sound. Her stockinged feet shifted, half-lion, half-woman. One knee bent and she stared at him, the fringe swinging. The lion beneath her began to rise and Leon realized it wasn't a rug.

Mr. Becker appeared and said, "Leon Shaffer, this is Lil Moore, the creator of the paintings. She's an artist of infinite promise and exquisite imagination." He bowed.

Smoke leaked from Lil's mouth and she coughed. She slid from the back of the lion, now almost standing. Its yellow eyes shone, the black-rimmed mouth half-open. Leon stepped back.

"It's Herbert's bedtime," Mr. Becker explained as he led the old, sad lion away, resting the palm of his hand on the tawny back. The lion yawned, showing yellowed teeth; his hide rippled. Flies scattered.

A hoarse voice emerged from the diminutive, dark woman in front of Leon, "Are you ready for something exciting?"

Chiaroscuro

"What is the body but a set of colors adjusting to canvas?" Alice asked everyone at the restaurant table. "Like the seasons," she added, fumbling with her oversized sweater, a bright red-knitted cap, and gloves where her fingers poked out. She wore the same outfit for *Vanity Fair* except that she had an umber scarf undone by the wind.

"Alice, you make it sound like something that must be manipulated. But it's already there, a landscape, a complete world in itself, and I should know." George Holman grinned boyishly, although he was well into his fifties, a gray mustache umbrellaed over his top lip. He knew he was handsome and he adored each woman in her own particular way. "Just paint what you see."

"And what was it that you saw in your nude photographs of Audrey, George? Lil, you remember Audrey poised against rocks with the lower part of her in that cold river?" Marco, the perpetual Latin American piano player asked.

"Yes, I remember his close-ups of Audrey's breasts breaking the water and photographed from above. It was titled 'Fish Clouding the Moon', right, George?" A waiter brought Lil white rice in a painted blue bowl. The steam obscured her youthful face, her red lips visible momentarily at the famous Round Table in the New York Chinese restaurant on Columbus Circle. There were only six people there that late Saturday night. The vast, white, round tablecloth, a fat, full moon, was between them. Alice Thompson with George, Marco with a light-skinned colored singer named Izzy, short for Isabelle, who had been singing since she was fourteen, and Lil was with Leon. It was late, yet a last dish of sweet and sour chicken was set down before them.

"I used glass plates and long exposures. It took three or four minutes, so the edges blended, but they became too soft." George believed that if his intentions were good, so were the results, and that no one would be harmed by his actions. "I don't take photographs anymore," he explained to no one in particular, shaking his head.

"Poor Audrey," Izzy whispered into Marco's ear, but they all overheard her.

Red paper lanterns with dragons were suspended over their heads. Two white, poodle-haired, ritzy-looking ladies sat in a cracked leather booth against the wall. Red carpet spread out under their feet. Smooth crimson menus with tassels were piled high on a nearby table. Curlicues of fog rose from their table and the smell of hot oil and ginger lingered in the air.

Lil lifted her chopsticks to her mouth. "What would the Dadaists do with a body?" Leon watched her. Izzy yawned, showing beautiful, white teeth, and she rested her dark head on Marco's shoulder. Her silver evening dress slipped lower over her small breasts.

"The torso would be constructed from curtains or silverware or other common household items." Alice's rough elbows rested on the table; her fork glared at their faces.

Lil thought she smelled something burning, the heavy,

sticky odor of rice in a hot pan. "And what would the Precisionists do with a body?"

"I can answer that," Alice said, having once painted several New York buildings as tall, angular shadows peering over the straight, flat streets below. "The body would be all form, geometrical shapes, and there wouldn't be a narrative point. It would be all aloof and emotionless."

"Much like Cubism, but without its multiple points of view." While the rice cooled George watched as Lil's face appeared from behind the steam. He looked at Alice, who took care of his needs, frowning with her ridged forehead, the lines etched stridently across her face. Destiny, he thought, was the tide laughing at us as all the debris from our past pulled us under.

"Those would look nice in your hair," Izzy said sleepily to Lil, pointing at the chopsticks hesitating at her mouth.

"Yes, perhaps they would. Eat, Leon." Lil held her chopsticks up, looking at them from different angles. She wondered if Leon was lost or bored with this conversation she found glamorous and necessary. Lil trembled under the reddened light, a dragon poised overhead, ready to pounce on wounded prey. She wondered if George would have called it a "moral shiver," for George certainly had the moral heebie-jeebies. Leon spooned some rice and eggs into his mouth and some bits fell off, staining the tablecloth. His hair stuck to his ears as he turned his head to listen to whomever was speaking. She imagined his lovers, secretaries too busy for more than an hour's lunchtime rendezvous, or the friend of an acquaintance, grateful for a sizzling steak dinner. Alice's fork flashed light into the horizon of Leon's gray eyes.

Lil glimpsed remoteness and an iris split with black. "What about the Futurists? What would their model look like?"

"Ah, all machines and motion, sharp edges and violence."George twisted his mustache into small ropes.

George was having too much fun, Lil thought. But I am too. It's funny how Leon's presence alters our conversation, makes it somehow less personal, more distant.

Alice removed her gloves and wiped George's mouth with a white napkin. He pushed it away, feeling suddenly either too young or too old.

Leon thought he would prefer to see a real nude model rather than the interpretation of one. He couldn't say that he was crazy about Chinese food either.

"How about the Negro Movement?" Izzy's head lifted and fell back onto Marco, lolling, her eyes closed and her thick lashes fringing her cheeks. "I don't know much about art, but that music sure can bring a body back from the dead. Jelly Roll, Eubie Blake, Armstrong. Do you know about them?"

George's mustache became energetic, gray wings flying on his face. "Sure, and how about William H. Johnson and Archibald Motley?"

Izzy sighed and fell into a silken heap against Marco's black shirt. Alice's arm inched over to George's animated hands and she held his fingers in her own. Together they resembled a fleshy beast writhing on the white table. It was an overtly awkward gesture. A waiter's soft shoes marched by, accommodated by the carpet, dark in spots like dried blood. Exhausted shadows crept by. George seemed calmer. He collapsed against the back of his seat as if wind had leaked from him. Lil lit up a cigarette and postured with her mouth and eyes. She was etched again in smoke, a charcoal sketch, a fading watercolor, hardly there. She inhaled. She poured something from a silver flask into her tea and drank it immediately. After she swallowed, she exhaled and smoke flew from her lips like a short scream.

"Are we saying anything new here?" Lil spit out, impatient and unhappy. "Maybe the Beckers' party drained us."

Marco laughed. His gold tooth showed. "Do we ever? Maybe we need some of the writers here tonight. Or have they already been here and left?"

"The Ku Klux Klan would liven things up," Izzy mumbled. "Believe me, I know."

"Oh, Izzy," Marco said, "no one can even tell that you're colored."

"That's why I don't get thrown out of these restaurants," she mumbled, half asleep. "But everyone knew me down South."

"We could get a two-dollar Mah Jong set from the drugstore down the street," Alice suggested.

"How about inviting Red Grange with his football?" Leon said, sipping some tea. He watched Lil in the periphery.

Leon, Lil thought, I nearly forgot about him again. Is his happiness my responsibility since I brought him here?

Jazz wandered from the kitchen as the door opened and closed. Lil had expected Chinese music. The poodle-haired ladies lurched from their booth, holding their palms against the red wall as if to comfort it. They unsteadily pressed the tabletop. They exited, zozzled, on straining high-heeled shoes. They wrapped thin, mink stoles around their necks. The shriveled, glass-eyed heads with snouts and teeth dangled over their chests. Lil blew some cigarette smoke in their direction. It bloomed around their backs.

Leon wasn't certain what being Bohemian was, but he believed that George, Alice, and Lil embodied it. Heroes and heroines? There was nothing about them that resembled boredom. It was all angry offerings, parts of the body, like the color red all hot and bothered and everywhere. He thought of learning to dance and shimmying with Lil. He believed George was too flamboyant and noticeably attractive. Here, with these artists, sex could be ignited over a stray collarbone. These friends fit together like music, original, sometimes dangerous, sometimes helpful. Not like the niceties he spent his days exchanging with people he had known for years. These people had revolutionary morals. He saw their good side.

"Let's move more deeply into our subconscious and forget about the body for a while," Lil said. When she spoke, she looked at George, who rubbed his left side, near his hip, with his hand, as though his kidney bothered him again. His face was a changing composition, at first all dark yellows, then paler, with pastels or the black, white, and gray of his photographs. Alice's face flew to concern for a moment and then smoothed out again.

Lil saw that being a Bohemian was a tornado stopped only by the largest, most solid house you could find. It was the boat that loved the water, which tried to drown the boat. It was permission.

"You've been through psychoanalysis, haven't you, Lil?"

Marco yawned, noticing Izzy's eyes were already closed. There was movement behind the curtains to the kitchen and then a noisy discussion broke out in Chinese as pots and pans banged, ringing loud, tinny songs. A waiter emerged gesturing, reciting something under his breath.

"I still see someone for psychoanalysis. He trained with Sigmund Freud," Lil said matter-of-factly, knowing what could become of that knowledge among this group. She thought of George tracing the curve of her neck, enjoying her body. Although it had been a while, the imperfect chronicle of time.

A waiter, who had already changed into his street clothes, tripped on the carpet on his way out the front door. He snarled something in Chinese to no one, for there was no one there who could understand him. Then he said in broken English, "Nifty. Just ducky."

Lil thought of Joan of Arc, who had done something new, an abberative creation. She had gone on alone, unbound by the rules of the land, and fought for what she believed in. She had tried to reach beyond her time and place. She had also heard voices that told her what to do. There was always some form of sacrifice in admiration.

"I know," Lil said, "a tribute to psychology." She crushed her cigarette in the empty rice bowl, then raised her teacup into the air.

"Is this like *Wit and its Relation to the Unconscious*?" George was aware of the dragon over their heads protruding from its lampshade. His hand dropped Alice's, which remained on the table like an unappetizing dessert.

"I keep on painting *The Psychopathy of Everyday Life*." Alice smiled. Her listless sweater, the color of rotted peaches, was shapeless.

Alice's red knit hat reminded Lil of slash wounds across Alice's forehead. Alice was lost in her clothing, her body found only by George in photographs or on their big, metal frame bed that Lil didn't want to think about. Alice was cowardly, except in her paintings.

Izzy's wild hair mottled the light dappling Marco's cheek. His gold tooth flashed. "I'm all for *The Interpretation of Dreams*." He closed his eyes.

"I'm just beginning the *Theory of Sex* myself," Leon piped up. He had started reading Freud and found much there to disgust him. It was clinical and told him more than he wanted to know. Leon preferred subtlety, such as walking up the narrow stairs of his apartment house and wondering whether he smelled sex from a married couple's window as their curtains blew tempestuously. He had never heard any sharp cries or rustling, although he listened sometimes. Perhaps they were only having dinner but he always imagined more.

Lil smiled at Leon, her cigarette smoke slipping around his ears. She wondered whether she should leave him there, misplace him like an old paintbrush. "Let's try something else. How about the word 'wish'? What do you immediately think of?"

"As in 'I wish I had money,'" George answered.

"That's good but just say 'money,'" Lil cajoled him, for they seemed to be her rules exclusively.

"More painting," Alice said, jutting her pointy chin out.

"Better. Try for one word."

"Songs. But I really want to say songs and more kissing." Marco looked dreamily at Izzy, who was sleeping slumped against his shoulder in a silver pile, her dress wrinkling. She snored gently.

"Fulfillment," Leon said.

"Ah, Leon understands," Lil said, believing it took years to get to the puzzle. Each person was a child's doll dressed up, sometimes cruelly, sometimes kindly. It was difficult to see behind their deceptions. Freud had the right idea, detective work that rooted out the sources. "Now try the word 'dream.'"

"Life," Marco mumbled. "What do you think of, Lil?"

"Want," Lil said. "Leon?"

"Wife," Leon blurted out, but felt embarrassed.

Lil moved around several grains of cooked rice that blended into the tablecloth with her chopstick. She couldn't consider this a still life, for there weren't enough different shapes and colors and she didn't let the rice stay still. She thought of a lovely bowl filled with rice, an exotic spoon, a red lantern with tassels, and a gold-stitched kimono piled onto a table. A Chinese still life. Different and brightly colored. "How about 'love'?"

But with that word everyone groaned. Marco and Izzy were nearly asleep. Alice swept crumbs from the table with her large, raw-boned hands. Her face seemed perched on someone else's body with its frail features, the detailed lines around her mouth and eyes as she peered downward. George idly pulled his watch from his vest pocket. Leon sat quietly, obediently looking at Lil. He could sense the haphazard trail of several automobiles outside, their overly bright headlights, the jarring honk of a horn, the clanking. The moon was round and whitely rising. A breeze lifted leaves from the cement sidewalks and tossed them against skyscrapers. Clouds, neither seen nor heard, were hidden behind buildings. Ribbons of stars were lost because of the shine from department stores and drugstores. The city was vibrant, never sleeping, similar to the Beckers' country house, which Leon and Lil had just escaped. Leon looked at Lil, who appeared to have poised her chopsticks in the air as she would have done with her cigarette holder, without thinking.

Lil was changing positions, posing. She was staring at a mound of raccoon coats left hanging on a coat stand near the door, remembering the day she had tried to take a raccoon for a walk at the Beckers' estate on Herbert the lion's leash. It was toward the end of one of their parties and the raccoon had at first complied as she fed it some food at dawn while the sun rose above the placid, reflecting lake. But then it turned on her and she had to throw the leash at it and run to the house. Mrs.Becker had insisted at that point that Lil try psychoanalysis, adding, "and because of all that had happened with George."

Lil had answered her, "But I adore animals, even more than men, and this was just one of my surrealistic tendencies."

Lil had uncharacteristically obeyed Mrs. Becker's request for analysis, later telling her, "Next time I might try dancing with a turtle or squirrel or a rat."

"Please, Lil dear, not here. Perhaps in the city. But how terribly Bohemian of you."

~

Grab a Peppy – instead of a bonbon!

I light a Peppy cigarette and eat less sweets. That's how I
keep in good shape and always feel lively.

It's toasted – no throat irritation – no cough. 45
minutes toasting develops its aristocratic flavor – mass
production makes its democratic price possible.

~

Leon opened his eyes to the morning light creating harlequin
designs on Lil's bedroom walls. Lil, however, was nowhere

to be found and her side of the bed remained untouched.

The previous night she had lain across her bed in the same way she had positioned herself on the lion. One hip rested on the thick wool blanket, her sheets bordered with tiny yellow flowers. Orange fringe swayed from the curving borders of her body. She had only four rooms in her walk-up and they were small. A bedroom, kitchen/dining room, living room, and a studio space that could barely fit a single bed along its white walls splattered with paint. Her paintings were stacked against the walls, and one, with bougainvillea gone wild, sat on an easel, flowers curling along the edges of the canvas. Splotches of dried paint dappled a palette. Closed tubes and jars, dripping different colors, lay on the cloth around the base of her easel. The ceilings were tall, and dark-veined marble decorated the entrance to all the rooms.

"Take off your clothes." Lil rose and went into the bathroom and ran a bath. She returned to the bedroom. "You can take them off in the bathroom, if you prefer," when he had hesitated.

Leon stepped into the bathroom and half shut the door, then slipped into the warm water in the deep, pink enamel bathtub. His toes climbed the opposite end, toward the faucets. Various parts of his body floated to the surface, depending on how he moved under the water. He thought of little boats scooting across the water. They submerged, only to resurface a moment later. This is enjoyable and quiet, he thought, after so many people, such a busy party. Then Lil came in.

"All clean?" she asked in her husky voice. She took off

her own clothes. He watched for a girdle, garters, or a bras-
siere. But there was only a pair of bloomers. Lil arranged her
dress carefully on a chair so the orange fringe swung to and
fro, sounding like someone sweeping the same spot over
and over again. Her body was lithe and flat-chested and an-
archical, with three small scars near her chest. It found space
between Leon and the bathtub and its water. Her body shifted, then sank and reappeared. They fit their parts together,
wet, splashing, and hurried. Leon wanted her so much he
was overeager. She flailed over him in half air and half water until they both cried out. Water dripped along the sides
of the tub. Lil's hair hadn't gotten wet but she brushed it.
Then she wrapped herself in a blue robe and disappeared,
the door creaking in her studio.

Leon dried himself slowly. Next time he would be prepared and take precautions. He went into her bedroom and
fell upon the design of embroidered yellow flowers and
then fell fast into a contented sleep.

When Lil peeked into the bedroom in the morning, she
was freckled with paint and smelled of linseed oil, turpentine, and the petroleum scent of paint. She wore an ostrich
boa over a thin nightgown covered with frazzled roses. An
empty paintbrush flicked in her hand, reminding him of a
cigarette. Her hair fell over her forehead and cheeks. The
dark circles under her eyes were a collision between night
and morning. "I have a terrible appetite for invention," she
said dramatically.

"Is that what you call not sleeping?" Leon laughed and
took a fistful of his clothing as the sun splayed itself along
his back. He thought of September as a month when school

started up again, when plants began to close up, showering their leaves on unsuspecting strangers, and of the odor of cider and wool, and how everything, including people, began to lose their depth and height to the wind. Air smelled burnt. Women cleaned their closets and brought out their gloves, coats, hats, and sweaters.

"People make too much of sleeping anyway." Lil didn't want to tell Leon about her sleepwalking incidents. When she did finally fall asleep a few months ago, she found herself outside a just-opening fruit stand. The owner was too busy to notice her standing by the apples in her nightgown, thank goodness. Or the time she woke up outside a speakeasy with drunks stumbling into her and finally knocking her awake. "My painting is insistent. Come and see what I've done with the bougainvillea, how it can never tell the truth."

"How does a painting lie?"

"It lies about reality in order to reach another truth. The same way lovers do." Her eyelashes vamped over her tired eyes.

Leon lay on the bed, the sheets and blankets rumpled into valleys and hills separated by crushed yellow flowers. He imagined being in an aeroplane, watching everything grow smaller, the landscape becoming a mere child's toy to be tinkered with. "You mean the way we try to look our best for the other person—and all that sort of thing?"

"Yes, aren't we just projecting who we want to be?" Her paintbrush clawed the air over Leon's legs.

"Yes, my little lioness," Leon folded her into his arms, "but you already know who you want to be."

"And who is that?"

"Mary Cassatt or Dora Carrington." He smiled. He wasn't dead to the world, he just couldn't spend a lot of time in it. He spent more time with numbers, symbols connected to a world of outer objects that weren't transformed by an inner process, the blank canvas of a large house, good silverware, a functioning automobile. He was modern. People still translated money into other things, dreams, marriage, and a good life. This was not his concern, most of the time, these interpretations. But these transformations were everything to Lil.

She smiled, but was this necessary? This getting to know each other. Most men didn't know much about language, the words made into sentences. It all felt like stray colors, a complicated composition to them. It defied their ordinary negotiations, a strong wave pulling them too far underneath. He was staring at the curve of flesh above her nightgown, one that he had traced with his tongue last night. He had counted the minutes, demanding her pleasure and she, grudgingly, had obliged.

She had thought about George's dirty photoflood lamp and his camera on a rickety tripod, and how she had unwittingly pushed them with her feet during sex with George until they were broken and unusable. He had said, "Finally, I'll capture a woman on paper." That was before Alice.

"Instead of clouds," she had replied.

"No, along with clouds because clouds are women."

Lil didn't know what he had done with the photographs of her. She hadn't ever seen them.

At that moment she was certain that art would drink up her whole life, the way a river carved the earth into what it needed. She studied George's face in her hands, the tufts of white hair in his ears, the loose flesh on his bones, his mustache that swept everything up, the wrinkles that said, *Forget me, I'm already gone.*

Another night when she had painted George there was a storm in New York that howled at the windows, struggled with the few remaining trees, knocked at her door, screamed its outrage, and brought down the electric wires so she had to use candlelight. The result was a confusion of color, George looking over his shoulder at the noise, fatigued, a collapsed perspective. He looked as if he were evaluating a child he was uncomfortable with. As if he wanted to say: *Call me when you have learned something, when you have grown up.*

"I don't believe I'm anyone's lioness." She knelt at the bed. "The Beckers confided to me that you're an orphan too."

Leon wanted to see her again. He wanted to answer her precisely. "Yes, my mother and father died in a boating accident when I was thirteen. I was sent to live at my aunt's house in Iowa before I moved here."

"No brothers or sisters?" She stared at the window beyond Leon and the morning arriving behind the almost bare trees.There were busy sidewalks below filled with men in dark overcoats, tweed, two-toned shoes, women with large, gray droopy hats, coats and matching silk shoes.

"No. And you?" He wanted to kiss her again, to memorize the bones in her fingers and have them touch the clandestine parts of his body. Again. But he knew that the next time she would have to come to him.

"I have an older brother in Chicago that I haven't seen in a long time. He was gone when I was growing up." Her face was silhouetted. Her mouth dissolved in the light, although she was still talking. "My mother died eleven years ago, when I was fifteen. I never knew my father." She reached under her bed and removed some men's knickerbockers and climbed into them. They were shapeless and too big over her knees. Lil thought briefly of the clothes Alice wore in public. Lil's face was hidden in the ostrich feathers and her nightgown was a bulge along the top of the knickers. "Do you want to see my new painting?"

"I can't. I have to go to work. I'll have to see it another time." Leon rushed for his watch. His socks and shoes were under the bed. "Well, I'm sorry to hear that you're also an orphan," he said to Lil.

"See you later, alligator," she murmured, turning back toward her bougainvillea, which she knew couldn't hurt her.

~

"An Experiment in Modern Music" Has Mixed Results

Paul Whiteman's band, including Mr. Gary Gray on clarinet, Joe Venuti on violin, and George Gershwin, the composer himself, on the piano, played at Aeolian Hall in New York City last night. The event was scheduled as an "educational" concert including such movements as the

"True Form of Jazz." Mr. Gershwin's "Rhapsody in Blue" received an unenthusiastic premiere. Mr. Gershwin wrote the piece in three weeks and it showed. Even though the 60 piece orchestra had Ferde Grofe as its leader and the opening glissando by Mr. Gray was inspired, much of the piece was aimless and formed of short, jumpy segments. The cadenzas and tuttis were too long and there was too much sentiment in the harmony. Mr. Gershwin nevertheless showed some talent and there was heartfelt applause from an audience tired from a lengthy concert and a broken ventilation system.

~

As Lil entered the room there was the same long, gray velvet couch with one pillow, the intrusive leaves of a nearby ivy plant, the vacuous window. Dr. Duncan tapped his pencil repeatedly on his desk when he was making a point, a restless, American gesture.

It was all too predictable—the past Lil returned to at least once a week. The Beckers had been paying for it now for over two years. It was spoken of only in the same hushed tones as discussing paintings or religion. Lil tried to imagine how Picasso thought up "Les Demoiselles d'Avignon," the shattering of all conceptions that went before it with the asymmetrical, flat bodies, color and light draped like broken shards around them. It was like a religion. Mrs. Becker had been analyzed. "And I came out the other end of it," Mrs. Becker proudly said, "even better."

Dr. Duncan wore a white linen suit most of the time

that made Lil want to scream about convention until she discovered the lavender, orange, and sky-blue shirts hidden underneath. The same dark tie always half-heartedly covered them, these colorful secrets. His hair was nearly white, although Dr. Duncan wasn't particularly old. It was an office room among many where Lil and Dr. Duncan were supposed to pray, pry, explain, deny, and discover at least once a week, Thursdays at 3:00 p.m. at East 52nd Street, on the second floor of a coal-stained brownstone building.

Session. Fragment of an Analysis of a Case of Sublimation: Lillian Moore.

Patient lies on her side on the couch, then lies on her back with her hands folded, as if obediently. Patient is wearing a gray crêpe-de-Chine dress with black dots. Her expression is tired or spiritless, or both. Note to self: what is she sublimating?

Patient: I want to see my life at a distance, on a canvas.

Doctor: What about living it?

Patient: I want to separate it from me, become bougainvillea.

Doctor: Why bougainvillea?

Patient: Because they're lilac and red and spread wildly and take to the jungle and tropics. They're exotic and adaptable.

Doctor: Are they like you?

Patient: They have the same symptoms, if that's what you mean. (Patient turns her head toward analyst.)

Doctor: What are your symptoms right now?

Patient: Insomnia, some nerves, and my fingers were numb for three days, but then it went away.

Doctor: So tell me, how is the bougainvillea like you?

Patient: They don't sleep and they keep me company at night. They're a nervous red and purple, but I don't know if they're ever numb. I'll have to ask them. (Patient's hands fall to her sides.) They want to live life to its fullest or not at all. To blossom or die. How perfectly negligent and American is that?

Doctor: You haven't had any dreams lately because of your insomnia?

Patient: No, you'll be the first person I tell if I have any.

Doctor: Has anything unusual happened?

Patient: A man in a luncheonette asked me if I wanted to be in the moving pictures.

Doctor: What did you tell him?

Patient: That he was a crazy fish. I wondered if he was tipsy but he bought me lunch and seemed on the level. He said I should enter a beauty contest first.

Doctor: Are you going to?

Patient: I don't know yet.

Doctor: Your time is up.

(Patient is standing.) Patient: And I slept with someone new last night. (Patient departs.)

Impasto

That afternoon the streets were wet and slick with liquor spilled from a bootlegger's truck. Wind picked up mottled leaves and sifted through them. Buildings rose oblivious to the weather, blind to the cars, which were all curves and bright chrome punctuated by windows. The cars, windshields pasted with stray leaves, honked or paused to see what life was flying by. Cars loved the world, the emptiness they pushed through. Cathedral bells rang and a record inside an apartment sang to anyone who would listen. Leon held Lil's arm as they exited the subway station with its rush of metal-tinged air, the loud, grinding sound that followed them as they left. A crowd halted, enclosing them for a moment at the top of the stairs. They contentedly watched as an elevated train, a trolley, several yellow cabs, and a horse pulling an ice truck passed them. They didn't even try to talk over the noise. A traffic light blinked green and all the people crossed the street.

Lil and Leon walked by shops. A jewelry storeowner had a man by his collar and threw him outside, upsetting a grocer's stand of onions. Apartment buildings cast ornate shadows that Lil and Leon stepped on. At one curb an empty bottle rattled against a sewer grate. The couple soon reached one of the largest buildings downtown, the Shelton Hotel at Lexington and 49th. Their necks strained as they tilted their heads, trying to see the top of the building.

Lil imagined men, women, and children cut down by stuttering Thompson submachine guns the way they did it in Chicago, against the brick walls of available buildings. A mother was caught in the crossfire with her wailing infant. Another woman carried a basket of groceries that became a colorful mosaic at her dead feet. One of her shoes flew off and came to rest in the gutter. Dying men twitched and clutched their chests. Their hats, incredibly, remained on their heads. The bystanders were relieved when the terrible noise was over, inspecting forlorn parts of their own bodies for damage, grateful that they were still alive. The innocents, caught in the crossfire, were sacrifices that were made in ancient times to angry gods. Just like in the tabloids.

After Lil and Leon entered the building a uniformed man in the lobby announced their impending arrival into a private telephone. They took an elevator and the elevator man told them when they reached the thirty-second floor. Alice and George's apartment was square and white, with too many angles, aquatic with an intrusive flowing light. The apartment contained very little furniture. The view was lovely but competed with the paintings and photographs on the walls. They sat and a round of highballs was offered.

"To Alice's successful show at the Armory last week." George lifted a glass that reflected black and white rectangles, the gaping windows of the nearby high-rises. "Leon, we're glad you could join our little celebration."

Lil stood by the window peering down at the miniature trees that steadfastly held onto their remaining leaves. Lil wondered why they persisted so in the face of difficult weather. Like so many actions, she thought, you can't help doing. Was their persistence a form of repair or resistance? She wore an intricate pale pink chiffon dress that crinkled as she moved. As she sipped from her triangular glass, she watched a tiny line of motor cars inching down the street. "It's nifty being up so high. Everything at a distance seems so suddenly small and different." She could see down Tin Pan Alley.

"You'll have to try painting the New York skyline from up here," Alice commented. "George and I shouldn't be the only privileged ones." She wore linen pants and an over-large cream-colored sweater. Her dark hair was pulled back severely. Silver bracelets jangled on her left wrist, speaking as she moved.

"By the way, when can I get something more from you, Lil? I want to do a women's exhibit at my 191 Gallery this winter." George laughed and his throat moved up and down, his mustache jumping. "All four of you women artists."

Leon sat on the plain brown sofa. He felt something stirring at the center of Lil's crinoline, something about to burst like the explosion of flowers in the center of George and Alice's wooden coffee table. The architecture of the city had unsettled Lil.

"I'll do a portrait for you as soon as I'm done with my commission for the Beckers." She twirled around, her dress erasing George. "Whose portrait do you think it should be?" Her dark bob covered her eyes.

"Alice's," George answered without hesitating.

Leon turned his head to the window, watched a woman in red lingerie haughtily washing her dishes in another building. Her body was cut into pieces between the red swatches of cloth. She scrubbed efficiently, lingering over the spots. Her dark hair drifted across her face in waves. She stood up straight, wiped each dish dry with condescension. In another apartment window a young boy played with wooden trains. They ran around and around his crossed legs. Knickers ballooned at his knees. Leon could see the boy's mother in another room trying on hats. If the boy had cried, she would have leaped up and bounded into his room. How different the world is for all of us, Leon thought. Leon wondered how George could afford the apartment. Lil scowled, trying to disguise it with a forced smile.

"When you don't sleep," she explained, "everyone seems unappealing. Everything gets all balled up."

"How about doing Leon's portrait?" Alice asked. She thought that Lil was one of those artists that painted her toenails crimson one day and then the next day scornfully removed the polish. Lil was still young. Perhaps she just wanted George again.

Alice had seen this before, but the women that helped at George's gallery were usually older and married. Their necks were scented with lavender or musk, they wore too much make-up and their hair was done a little too elaborately. Their mouths formed endless sighs. For them, George was a form of fiction, another escape among motion pictures, teas, luncheons, benefits. When the women realized George had forgotten them for a new sculpture or mural or sketch, they left. They could find that inattentiveness at home.

But Lil was the kind of woman who repeated herself until she was heard. She was still pretty, although Alice supposed that she was the type that cried as she painted at night instead of sleeping. A wound that could bleed forever. Alice had heard the rumors about her, along with everyone else. She had also heard that Lil once bludgeoned a young artist's painting into fragments at the gallery, saying, "I don't want to subject anyone else to this." The young artist cried and Lil pieced it back together differently. "Look," Lil pointed at the new painting, "it's better."

Alice could see that Lil's pain intrigued George. She could see him saying to Lil, "I insist you suffer for more paintings."

"I hate romantic portraits. They're so insipid," Lil stated, noticing the tart odor of turpentine lingering in the room.

"Then don't do one," George replied, his finger idly stirring the surface of his drink so that his reflection became rippled and distorted.

They watched darkness arrive from behind tall buildings, churning among clouds, backlit like a famous movie star making an entrance, muting everything for a moment. Then the electric lights in the buildings switched on as automobiles threaded their way through the streets below. They could see clearly into the apartments that had not closed their curtains yet. They could see lives tinkering on, their mundane tasks not yet completed. Lives expressed in mindless gestures. Leon knew that a person could be lonely in this city where so much happened. The lit windows spoke across the distance.

George took Leon aside. "I don't know how serious you

are about Lil, but they say she stabbed someone," George whispered. "I don't know anything more than that. She doesn't talk about it. It's just a warning."

"I'll keep that in mind, although I'm certain she had her reasons," Leon said.

George laughed. "Some men find that kind of mystery appealing and challenging." He turned away.

In the darkened room, Alice explained to everyone, "I only do enormous paintings of fruit."

"Stay with me a while, until you're tired and want to go to sleep," Lil said in her studio.

Leon watched her, but there wasn't much to see. Dabs of light brown around a blue, abstract figure. He looked over her head. She used a small knife and a brush, adding colors on top of the blue and brown, until a figure emerged, surrounded by green. He observed her hands, which seemed to be moving along unpredictably. He wasn't sure whether staring at her incomplete art was a step forward or backward, but his eyes tired of the light.

"For these oil paintings I stretched the linen canvas over wood boards, and the sizing was made from rabbit skin glue to seal the pores." She looked over at Leon, wearing his pajama bottoms, as he leaned against his chair, his cheek resting against his fist to show that he was trying to listen, his yellowish hair uncombed.

"After a day or two I mixed white lead with a little turpentine and let that dry on the canvas. Then I sanded it." She looked over again; he was nearly asleep, curling into the

back of the chair, his limbs loose over the sides, his almost
handsome features slack.

Lil listened to the sporadic, late-night traffic. "Every
once in a while I use watercolors or gouache or egg tempera.
And that's another type of preparation." She would have to
wake him up and guide him back to bed. Sometimes she felt
a bit weary, but then that, too, disappeared.

"Out of chaos comes painting," she murmured to the
painting itself.

"Does it need chaos?" Leon mumbled, his head falling.

A bright, red color appeared on her brush without her
having thought about dipping her brush into it. "You don't
understand," she muttered. "You really don't understand,"
she said to the lights outside, to the passing car wheels that
sounded like rain.

At George's gallery Lil considered what she would wear for
the beauty contest, because she "wouldn't mind" relinquish-
ing herself to the moving pictures. One of her friends knew
an agent who went back and forth between Hollywood and
New York. He had been interested in Lil ever since her friend
described Lil's beauty and flair for the dramatic, her per-
sonality. The agent wanted to see Lillian Moore in a beauty
contest. After all, acting was easy money, she hoped. A new
young married gallery attendant in a bruise-colored dress
with black ribbons braided into her russet hair fussed with
a bronze sculpture, then dusted a Braque. The woman wandered through the gallery as though it were an avant-garde
obstacle course. Finally, she settled into a chair to help any

visitors that dared to come.

"Do you remember," Lil exclaimed just loudly enough, "when you and Audrey and I went nude bathing out at the Becker's house two summers ago and that plainclothes policeman caught us and fined us ten dollars each for depravity?"

"How could I forget?" George straightened a framed sketch on a table. "Except Audrey wasn't there. And I paid the tickets." He was absorbed in his gallery, sorting, picking up a magnifying eyepiece, running it along the lines, his mustache twitching slightly like a little whiskered animal.

The attendant's sheen of red hair twisted as she eavesdropped on their conversation. Camouflaged in the intense gallery light, her lips glistened as she wet them. Her hands delicately crossed with her wedding ring resting on top. A dog barked outside and she leaped from her chair. She strode past Lil and George, noticing the fragile nature of his bent back, his tamed gray hair, the sketches and photographs at his table that his large, gentle hands rested on. This Lil, a visiting artist, was a sideshow, all glass bracelets and earrings that jarred, an old, red dress like something dangerous, yet playful. She had a wild bob and a grating voice. She didn't seem to know about soothing a man like George, older, tired, or how invisible women were the ones that arrived at an incident first, the ones who had learned their way around intimately and who appeared indispensable at just the right moment. It was like taking care of children.

Lil laughed. George's photographs of clouds hung on a wall between them. "Yes, you're right. Later we discovered how the policeman had been called by neighbors and had stood by the lake day in and day out for a week, just waiting to catch us. It was ludicrous."

"Have you begun working on your portrait for me yet?" Lil turned away, fidgeted with the corner of a photograph. "No, not yet. Don't you have two older paintings of mine?" Lil absentmindedly stared at a sleek orb centered on a stand in the large square space with an assortment of paintings, photographs, and sculptures around it. Her mind flew to the shapes, the distance of rectangular pictures, the curves of hanging masks and ritual pieces, the sticks and stones, metal nests and flowers, a visual puzzle, the horizontals, verticals, diagonals, all complicated and pleasing. The gallery was a body made of parts, all different, all graceful. An arm was moving, cleaning up the dirt that Lil tracked in, the woman's hand moving in wider circles. Lil shaded her eyes with her palms in order to see the woman in the overhead light, which was stronger above the works of art. Each painting displayed its details, asserting itself boldly.

George went to the small room in the back, where canvases were stacked in racks. Lil followed. Lil respected George's opinions about art. George stood before a figurative painting, not one of Lil's. There was only enough space for two people. "They're in here somewhere." He searched through a stack above him and pulled out a painting of glass jars filled with spices, and then one of a fierce model whose face was full of blotches. She wore only a strand of pearls that dipped near her breasts. "These?"

Lil turned away from them. They were already abandoned. She had forgotten the awkward lines, the colors that bled into one another, that became muddy. She ran a flame red fingernail along George's old jacket. "No, I'll give you a new portrait." She didn't say whose. She wanted an unraveling. She could love a time or a place more easily than a person. Although she thought about George often.

"Good." He removed her hand. "You know I'm with Alice."

"And with who knows who else." Lil tried to see where the swanky, married woman had scurried off to, but she didn't see the blur of her anywhere. She would be tidying or doing some paperwork. George took so much, until there was nothing more. She thought, I'm really no different from that new woman, busy somewhere under the feverish lights.

"What about Leon? He seems to be an amiable young man." George didn't look at her.

"Persistent."

"Who does that remind me of?"

But Lil turned to view a dark undulation in the gallery that came closer.

Izzy, dressed in a muslin suit, wandered toward them. Her dark, curly hair cascaded down her neck, her white teeth visible in a wide smile. She said, "Don't be sore at me, but I was nearby listening to Marcus Garvey speak and thought I'd stop by. The Universal Negro Improvement Association and African Communities League is right next door."

"I could hardly be angry with you," George said, lacing his arms through Izzy's and walking with her. Her heels clicked on the hard floor and resounded in the room. "Let me show you around. Now tell me about this Garvey. He's the Moses of the Negroes and wants the American Negro to return to Africa, isn't that right?"

They stood in front of a Marsden Hartley that was all hills and curves piled in layers of beige, brown, and green. The clouds were pure white petals. "Yes, that's right. Garvey wants a Black man o' sorrows.'" She hesitated. "I just don't know what he'd do with a Black woman o' sorrows." She smiled. "And, as usual, everybody stared at me there like 'what's this white woman doing here?'" Izzy had gotten used to that. "It's getting hard to fit in anywhere," she sighed.

"Not for someone as lovely as you." He wanted to change the subject. "I remember the Chicago riot in 'nineteen. There were so many injured and dead." George turned her toward the painting. "Isn't this lovely? It reminds me of you."

Lil left them there. Love is a forgery, she thought, an approximation of what you really want. She began to stride down the stairs and ran into Leon.

"What are you doing here?" She was startled.

"George invited me to the gallery and I was curious. I was hoping to find you here and take you out for lunch." He had already tried her apartment.

"Izzy's upstairs. She just stopped by." He was in his unfashionable work suit and hat. He was cheerful.

"Let's invite her along. And George too," he offered. Lil was dressed in a wide, red dress. Her small face was suddenly lit with the promise of an idea. He watched her features as a thought occurred to her.

"Wait here a moment. I'll go up and get them. I need to ask somebody for a favor," she said mysteriously to the stairs. She had a sudden idea for a model for her portrait. It would be another secret. She hurried up the stairs, the wood creaking softly under her weight.

~

Valentino in "Monsieur Beaucaire"

Rudolph Valentino, "Latin Lover" and film star of "The Sheik" (1921) and "Blood and Sand" (1922), has opened in a new film titled "Monsieur Beaucaire." The movie was negotiated by Natacha Rambova, Mr. Valentino's second wife. Mr. Valentino plays the lead, the Duke of Chartres of the court of Louis XV. The audience mainly consisted of swooning women. Several men left the theatre in disgust, although one man's hair was greased back into a "Vaselino." This reviewer, however, grew increasingly tired of the mannerisms, complicated costumes, and heavy make-up as well as the belabored plot.

~

They settled on a Harlem club that Izzy was going to sing in that night. It was a large, dark room with candles and low lights. There weren't many people there yet, just scatterings at the small, white tables. The waitresses wore elegant black and white uniforms, with a few frills and large patches of lace. They had a complicated choreography, one for selling cigarettes, one for drinks, then the food.

"How is the economy doing all around?" George asked Leon.

"Very well."

"These new department stores seem to have everything all laid out. They're full of handbags, dresses, scarves, and jewelry." Izzy tipped her head so that she could see the stage, adjusting to it. "And men's clothes too."

Leon laughed. "Yes, the stores are doing quite well."

"What do you care, George, you old Red? You haven't cared since the Wall Street bombing." Lil tilted her glass toward her lips.

George had already finished his steak and potatoes. "I want my gallery to survive."

"Maybe I can look at your books sometime," Leon offered.

"That might help," George said. A low singing voice reached him. He didn't know the singer, whose voice slipped between the tables. Her words described impending heartbreak. Izzy simply smiled with her beautiful teeth.

"I'll go and retrieve Marco and be back for the night," Lil said, pushing her chair out. Her small, lovely body was rising and her eyes avoided Leon. Her red dress expanded to fill all the space around her empty chair.

"I have to go back to work." Leon stood up, couldn't catch Lil's eyes. He wasn't invited to stay after all. He left through the club's revolving doors. His image appeared twice in the spinning framed glass, going and then coming back, but in reality he didn't return.

Outside the sky was white, blending into the backs of buildings. There was gray cement, the brick and stone of buildings, and finally the horizon and sky in layers. Autumn colors everywhere. Everything empty and smudged.

An advertisement for Coca-Cola was painted on the side of a building. It said "Refresh Yourself" and showed a woman in a white dress offering a bubbling glass. A woman's thick-heeled shoe, its buckle still strapped, lay on its side on the edge of the sidewalk with several candy wrappers. A little boy in a sailor suit with polished shoes and a smaller girl wearing a striped pinafore walked by, hand in hand, all by themselves. Leon wore an overcoat, his wrists dangling from the cuffs as if he were growing by the minute.

Lil put her arms through her yellow sweater with smoke-colored buttons.

"Poor Leon," Izzy said with a clucking in her melodious throat.

Leon was still on the periphery. He was all wet. Lil would be at the club tonight; she would call him if she wanted him, that was all. What would she want him for? There were so many interesting men around, even the bootleggers offered a dark, frightening kind of fun, a form of forgetting that could be attractive, a harshness that many women found fascinating. And he wasn't an artist or Bohemian of any kind. Could sums be artistic?

Alma, his secretary, was long gone from the office when he arrived. With her red lips, smartly bobbed hair, the bracelets that clacked with aplomb, he would have to ask her one day, nicely, what she was looking for, what kind of man she wanted. Leon knew she went to parties. Everyone did. Some mornings she was too tired to talk, her eyes blistered and dark, her skin sour, smelling like liquor. She moved slowly and grunted or nodded at everything he said. The telephone on her desk alarmed her when it rang and often her hand shook, trying to hold the heavy receiver.

Leon had tried to talk to her about the race riots, the Volstead Act, even the Dempsey fight, but she didn't appear to be interested in current events. He overheard her talking to her girlfriends on the telephone about kissing or a pair of stunning leather gloves, a silk scarf she wanted, a trip to France. There was a brochure about Paris that she kept hidden in her top drawer. He guessed that she would probably never visit there. She was hardly a heroine. She enjoyed the mass consumption Leon saw all around, with an emphasis on the mass. She only read the entertainment section of the newspaper.

Leon had heard the rumor that a drunk Lil had dragged Herbert the lion on top of one of the Beckers tables at a party and they had tried to dance until they both fell off. This was after George had left her. If that was Bohemian, then everyone was Bohemian in 1924.

Leon sat in front of a large, open book, his ruler lying along a row of numbers separated by blue lines. He hadn't turned a page in half an hour. His pencils sat patiently in their black cup zigzagged with a silver lightning design. They looked like they could fly on their own power. His lamp provided the only light in the office, a smoky, bloated light that faded along its edges. He was waiting for an idea, for a sign. He shifted in his office chair and it murmured under his weight. He looked out his window into the windows across the now quiet street. All the businesses were closed and dark, except one to the right where a man was emptying wastebaskets. Leon ran a hand through his blonde, wavy hair and thought: maybe I should treat her rough, the way a sailor would.

The telephone rang and Leon jumped as Alma would have the morning after a particularly lively night out, and then he composed himself and answered it.

"Hello, Leon Shaffer here."

A man's voice. "I know it's you, Leon. That's why I called. Listen, we need to set up a date and time for you to look at my books like we talked about."

"Yes, fine, George." Leon could hear voices, music in the background. "Just come on in anytime," he said, not thinking about what he was saying. He tried to hear if Izzy was singing. He wondered if Lil was there.

When he hung up he was sorely disappointed. No one had invited him to the club. He opened his accounting books instead. He knew he could make sense of the columns if he wanted to. Yes, he thought, he'd try treating her like some gangster's moll.

Lil had so much to do, her friends were knocking at her apartment door bringing news or gossip or something drinkable or something to eat, sandwiches or some exotic buns from a new neighborhood Russian bakery. She thought of Herbert the lion, and his dazzling, delicate face and how he asked for too little, and Leon, who asked for too much. There was the upcoming beauty contest, costumes and bathing outfits, hair rinsed with lemons and beer, smiles that were all show, and cheeks made rosy. Lil hoped the cameras would understand. They did for Ruth Malcomson, Miss America of 1924. The crowd on the new Million Dollar Pier in New Jersey had waited five hours for the judge's decision that day.

She had just begun the portrait for George. She opened the door to her studio and the woman, her new model, was sitting patiently on a chair. She thought about asking the woman to remove all her clothes, just to see if she would. Lil believed that she would, so she didn't ask her. Lil wanted her to scream and break objects. Lil wanted to tell her that wild horses were born brown and later some turned white, everything eventually becoming something else.

"By the way, what's your name? I forgot to ask you when I ran back into the gallery the other day."

"Mary Beach." Her apple-red hair brimmed at her shoulders, twisted around green ribbons, daring Lil to paint her.

"Have you modeled for any other artists from the One-Nine-One Gallery?"

"No, you're the first to ask me. I ain't been there long. You got to tell me what to do." Her fingers shook a little as she reached for the back of her chair.

Lil smiled to herself. Mary looked smaller, sitting still there in her studio, not furiously cleaning or tossing around paperwork, not kissing George at the end of the day in a back room somewhere. Her eyes were less green as they fixed on Lil, who was a whirlwind circling her, searching for the right angle.Mary was perfect to be tossed among the bougainvillea, her face peeking out. People were in one large garden on the brink of destruction. Mary was younger than Lil, but she was at the age that fattened young girls and sent them searching in their mirrors for the remnants of their younger selves.

"What does your husband think about all this?"

"Oh, he don't know from nothing and what he knows he don't approve of. But that ain't going to stop me." Mary knew that this larger-than-life, pretty little woman was a good painter, the real McCoy. George had told her so, and she believed he was on the up and up. That Alice was also a fine painter, but was too demanding of George's precious time. Mary understood strangled relationships. She had seen both of these women's paintings at the gallery. Alice's were large, languid fruit in sullen colors that faded into the background. The apples, pears, and oranges pulsed, vanished, reappeared. They were sensual revisions of food. Some were larger than the viewer's torso. The textures varied: rough oranges, corrugated bananas, the cautious red skin of apples. Lil's paintings were astonishments, stars that were propaganda eclipsing the night sky, tree branches embossed with leaves, a figure twirling into nothing, becoming the white blankness of the paper. They were different, but deep and lovely. That was the reason she was here. She liked Lil's work, and she was curious what the talented Lil would do with her.

Lil smiled again, took up her paintbrush and dipped it into white. She positioned herself in front of the bougainvillea. She could have escaped to the tropics. But now came the figure or the face hidden in all that lushness, which was working its way through the vegetation with enthusiasm. She would have to finish this one for herself and then do a separate portrait of Mary. She dipped her paintbrush into a mixture of brown and red and a little blue. Her hair, Lil thought, I must capture that lovely hair. "George will be surprised."

"You made me swear not to tell him," Mary said. "That way, you said, I'd be your discovery."

What a perfect thing to say. "Now remove your clothes."

Mary slowly took off her dress and slip and sat in her camisole, stockings, and shoes. She was full-figured with round breasts and a curving stomach. Her hair was messy in the snaking ribbons. Her escaping flesh was tender and smooth and vulnerable.

"No, I need all of it." Lil handed her a flat, green bottle.

Mary gulped several times from the bottle, hesitated, and then removed all the rest of her clothes. She handed the bottle back to Lil, whose tiny, dark features relaxed as she distractedly placed the bottle on the floor. Mary sat down again and Lil looked at her, a river of shadows gathered at her throat and thighs.

A white scar was a seam down her left hip. It meandered, raised and knotty. Lil thought of her own small scars and the other women that had helped George, and none would have posed for a painting. They were silly society women waiting for their children to visit them from schools or jobs, waiting for the next benefit. Two had been European; three had been lit with new, bottle-blonde hair. Lil dreaded the sound of heels on the gallery floor, suspecting there was a new woman assistant coming closer. The new cat's pajamas. One had laughed too much and too loudly, one had never learned how to read, one coughed up blood. They left at the end of the gallery shows, some lasting longer than one month, some much shorter. Most were called home by their husbands.

But Mary seemed different, not a disguised bluenose. She was grave and silent.

Mary's hand shivered against the chair back. Lil could feel the lure of Mary's soft face. And Mary had color, her dimensions mythical, rich.

"Can I bring my little girl, Beatrice, next time? I ain't going to leave her at home with those killjoys again."

"How old is she?"

"Six."

"Yes, please bring her. Okay, you can put your clothes back on for now," and that's when Lil began to paint her.

~

Charlie Chaplin Weds 16-Year-Old!

Charlie Chaplin and Lita Grey, an American actress born in 1908, were married secretly in Mexico last week to avoid possible imprisonment and scandal. Lita Grey is Mr. Chaplin's second wife. She played the Angel of Temptation in Mr. Chaplin's film "The Kid"(1921) and she was to be the lead in the upcoming film "The Gold Rush." However, it is believed that the new Mrs. Chaplin is with child and will therefore be unable to star in the new film.

~

The theatre was a good place for insects to die. They piled in corners. Window sills displayed tiny hills of them along the walls. The burlesque stage with thick, forest-green curtains was still empty when the theatre began filling up. Steam heat sputtered from the radiators.

Leon sat in the middle of the large, warm room waiting for the beauty contest. He had driven to New Jersey in a neighbor's borrowed Studebaker. He had puttered by a billboard for Pond's Cold Cream and Vanishing Cream that began "Dancing the morning..." and then he had motored past it, unable to read the end. He remembered the tin sign for Atwater Kent radios because it was a still life with blue and orange flowers, and he had wondered, for the first time in his life, whether the artist who made it had received enough compensation.

He waved at Izzy and Marco who were seated in the back on folding chairs, but he was thinking about Marx and Kandinsky and Freud, what each of them would have thought of this pageant. Disgusting (a flagrant display of materialism); colorful and emotional; and sexual. In that particular order.

Lil had laughed about the contest, saying, "Where else but in America would women take off their clothes for money and fame? I guess it's vaguely about beauty."

Last night at dinner Alice had said, "Everyone thinks they can buy beauty."

"But no one looks like me in the ads," Izzy snapped.

"Now, girls," Marco interrupted. "We men get to see you in all your finery." His gold tooth glowed. "Right, George?'

"I like women the way they are naturally. They don't have to win any contests."

All three of the women laughed.

Leon noticed a man with sharp features and a pointy nose in the front row, holding a program. His hair had an oily luster, including the hair growing from his ears. He held a pencil in each hand. Leon wondered whether he was the talent scout that Lil had mentioned and was hoping to meet. A girl with rolled-down stockings and rouge rubbed onto her knees sat next to Leon. She wore black galoshes. She whispered, "I want to be in the next contest, so I came to see if they were on the level. I want to be in the pictures. Have you been to one of these contests before?" Her voice was too high and garbled. It echoed inside his head, a tinny bird caught in a room that was too small.

"This is my first." He thought: Beware of what you admire and why.

"Are you cheering for someone?" he blinked at Leon with periwinkle eyes.

"Yes."

The plush curtains fell away and a woman walked out in a gown made of peacock feathers. The shimmering plumage swayed as she walked. The judges, two women among them, sat at the side of the stage. The man in the front row of the theatre, the talent agent, was taking copious notes. When the woman stopped at the front of the stage there were bright, bird-feathered eyes staring back at the audience. Several others clad in evening gowns moved about, but Leon sought out Lil and found her after about eighteen contestants. There was cheering and whistling and clapping from the back row when Lil appeared wearing high-heeled pointed shoes with a button on one side. Her shoes matched her sleeveless evening dress, which shone with gold flecks.

She already looked like a movie star to Leon. A reflective, golden aura radiated around her. Gone was her need to arrange things, her painting, the mystery of her stabbing, which hadn't worried him yet. Gone were the words or lack of them that could cause him agony. He had never seen her wear so much make-up before and her dark bob was perfectly manicured. Lil walked to the edge and winked at the man in the front row and then stood with the other women. Finally, another rhinestone-clad woman came out. Leon could hardly see her face amidst the glittering light that tossed around the room like confetti. She, too, was dazzling. Each woman was more glamorous than the last and Lil was near the end.

The man in the front row was intently scribbling. The bathing suit competition began and there was an eerie silence in the room. Leon could hear a judge turn a page, mark something with a pencil. The spitting of the overworked heaters along the walls punctuated the quiet. Most of the bathing suits were woolen, with straps. The outstanding ones had fringes and bows. One man yelled out, "That girl doesn't even know how to swim," at one of the contestants.

"She doesn't have to know how," someone else in the room answered.

The girl next to Leon sat transfixed as the bathing-suited women walked around the stage. One of the women judges ran up and measured the instep and fingers of one of the contestants. The girl next to Leon gulped air and swallowed. "It's close," she whispered, but her voice lifted up too high, screeching. Then all motion stopped. The fringe on a suit continued tapping. The echo of the last heeled shoe on the stage hung in the air. The colors grew sedentary. Leon wouldn't have noticed the colors before he met Lil. His heart reached out for her in her yellow bathing suit with its captive black belt and black trim. The bee's knees. She was tiny and distant, almost the size of a child. He had told her as meanly as he could that he couldn't see her for several nights. The sailor stance. It didn't work. She told him, "That's fine. I'm too busy anyway." And he hadn't heard from her.

Two names were called, and the women ran out from their semi-circle. Then Leon heard Lil's name and she stepped forward slowly, with either trepidation or dignity. He wasn't sure which. She took third place. There was clapping and shouting. The girl next to Leon trilled, "I heard that the police outside blocked a car of Ku Klux Klansmen from Hoboken. They've turned them away." When she rose he saw her stockings fall from her knees and she had to pull them up. Leon looked back but he didn't see Marco or Izzy any longer.

"I want a cigarette terribly." Then Lil was sitting beside Leon in a cloak that barely covered her bathing suit. She smiled. She wondered if she had lost something. She wasn't sure exactly what.

"Would you like some dinner?"

"No, I have to talk to the movie man." She nodded her dark head at his seat. She smiled again. "Third place. Not too bad for a Bohemian."

Thursday 3 pm Session with Lillian Moore. Notes on Sublimation Case with extreme insomnia: Will try idiosyncrasy (association) today. Patient likes Rorschach inkblots, says, "They are better than many of the paintings I've seen at museums and galleries."

Doctor: But what does this one remind you of? (Number 4)

Patient: Sex.

Doctor: And this one? (Number 11)

Patient: Death.

Doctor: This one? (Number 24)

Patient: Sex and death.

Doctor: No, seriously.

Patient: Seriously, to me, it's all form and shape. Their spatial relationship, how they sit on the page, interests me. That one, for instance, is close to the edge. Is it running away or is it falling off, losing itself?

Doctor: What do you think?

Patient: It stepped back for a better look and is falling over.It's going to fall off the page and land in your secret drawer.

Doctor: What do you see in this one? (Number 16)

Patient: Leaves from a branch. But then it also becomes a face about to rest on a shoulder. It's Kandinsky, and Hartley. (The patient lights one of her cigarettes.) Sometimes the images don't mean anything more than what they are. They just are. Sometimes they make a point about color or space. Or they tell a story. They can challenge your ideas. For instance, that one could be an example of randomness, an accident of life. (Patient sighs.)

Doctor: Why did you use the phrase "an accident of life"?

Patient: I don't know. It was probably something my mother used. Don't you want to hear about my contest?

Doctor: Yes, of course.

Patient: I came in third, but I'm going to get a chance at the moving pictures. I have a screen test in two weeks, here in New York.

Doctor: Good, good. Are you trying to prove something with the contest?

Patient: Maybe it's about the dough or being attractive enough to deserve attention.

Doctor: Now back to your mother. You haven't talked about her much in our work here.

Patient: That's because she killed herself.

Doctor: How?

Patient: I found her in our apartment.

Doctor: Yes. (A long silence.) We need to talk about the stabbing.

Patient: Some people want to get stabbed. And I do want to get better. But what about my painting?

Doctor: What about it?

Patient: I don't want it harmed.

Doctor: Don't you think you could paint if your life was more resolved?

Patient: I don't know. Patient stood, ending the session abruptly.)

The Halloween party at the Beckers' country house consisted of tents extending across their leaf-scattered lawn and wooden statues of painted Indians with a single stiff arm pointing outward with a sign attached to it that said, "This way." Arrows led partygoers to a large table with plain punch, tampered punch, and glasses filled from small, flat, deep-green bottles. Leon was an archaeologist complete with boots, slightly torn, dirty trousers, a thick, plaid shirt, and a rope hung around his neck. He carried a small pick, borrowed from the neighbor who had lent him the Studebaker, to keep his hands busy. He considered exposing long-buried treasures and the remnants of people's lives, turning them inside out, retelling their triumphs and mistakes. He could have gone as a newspaper reporter. Or a detective, unearthing loss. He hadn't rented any costumes before and the shops were all out by the time he had inquired. He wondered later what his neighbor could possibly be doing with a pick in New York City. He had looked up stabbings in the newspapers for the last several years but hadn't found anything about Lil.

He brushed by clowns, kings, queens, tattooed men, movie stars, several Egyptian princesses, one mummy, and a man in a cloak who was drinking his liquor straight from the bottle. He didn't see Lil. A man held onto the braided hair of a large "little girl" who led him from tent to tent. A ballerina danced by. A cowboy strode in circles with a group of old soldiers. Several people were dancing the Charleston near the house and one man's mustache fell off and fluttered to the floor. The air grew raucous and stirred fallen leaves into thin tunnels. A fur-trimmed cloak fell off a woman's shoulders. Leon wasn't sure if he would be able to recognize Lil. What would she be wearing? He hadn't talked to her in at least a week. I won't go to her, he thought, I'll wait until she finds me.

A Clara Bow duplicate walked by. The It-Girl was going to go and dip a toe into the Beckers' lake. Did Leon want to come along? Her dark hair was a storm cloud surrounding her face, which had a penciled beauty mark below her right eye. She wore a flowered scarf around her head and her skirt was slit up the front. They walked quietly on the hard ground, flattening the tired grass. It was colder outside. The party grew to a whisper behind them. At the lake they leaned against a damp tree. The lake surface reflected the far lights from the party. Leon smelled the fishy odor of the lake. The woman dressed as Clara Bow removed her sandal, immersed a toe, shattering some constellations floating on the lake. She shivered and slipped her bare foot back into her sandal. She gulped from a bottle and then passed it to Leon. He put his pick down and he drank.

"We all seem so happy," she said.

Leon didn't know what to say. They stared at the lights and stars sprinkled on the water. The trees grew darker, vanishing. He could smell her sharp, floral perfume. Edges around him became lost, blurred.

"My husband just ran away with some factory girl and I don't know where they went." She kissed his cheek lightly, unwrapping the rope from his neck. She moved her lips closer to his mouth. "It's so much easier telling a stranger."

"I have to go back to the party." Leon gently pushed her away from him. The strong perfume and liquor odor grew weaker. He grabbed his pick and left.

"I didn't mean anything by it," she said to his back that became smaller and smaller—the shrinking rope, the fading glint of his excavating tool. Gee, she thought, what a swell. Leon breathed deeply when he returned to a tent; he didn't have to think about that woman. He turned around when he heard a deep, hoarse, gasping sound over the inhalation of a cigarette. It was a man. He knew she was still there somewhere. A gladiator stepped out in front of him and Leon moved, bumping into a heavily jeweled Elizabethan queen whose tiara reflected light in a frenzy against his shirt.

"Oh, hello, Leon." Mrs. Becker seemed a bit ossified.

"Hello, Mrs. Becker. You haven't seen Lil, have you?"

"She's here somewhere." She looked about unsteadily.

"How is she dressed?"

She smiled crookedly. "Now that's for you to find out." She walked away, as best she could.

Mr. Becker, dressed as a king, swooped in, taking hold of Mrs. Becker's arm. "Isn't this a wonderfully irresponsible and irrepressible time?" They flew off.

There were too many heroines, movie stars, and queens at the party. Too many people seeking admiration and attention. Leon readjusted his rope, snaking it around his collar. Sometimes, he thought, you had to choose. His pick had become cumbersome, so he left it propped against a chair. He wanted to discover something. Dancers with stockinged feet knit the floors. Rum, vodka, and loud music were plentiful. The light apologized for everything. He wondered if Lil was looking for him. He wanted to see her fierce little eyes meeting his. She would stride in, see him, greet him with her hard voice. Leon closed his eyes and saw the lake spreading in increments, the woman with Clara Bow's hair asleep, drowning in it without having woken again. He startled himself with his misery. Laughter filled the tent. A clatter of heels, cars honking outside, glass muttering against glass. Leon saw Lil. Of course, he thought, that's her in the lion tamer's costume with Herbert ambling slowly by her side. Music from a live jazz band hurried around, moved toward Leon. Cigarette smoke rose from the old lion's dingy mane where Lil's hand rested as they walked. Leon's rope scratched at his neck. She wore trousers that puffed around her hips, hard-pointed shoes and a buttoned-down blouse with a snarling lion painted onto her back. Leon noticed this as she turned to say hello to Mrs. Becker, who was searching for a pebble in her shoe while she held onto her husband's arm. He had an urge to grab Lil, pull her toward him, hold onto her and keep her. But he knew she would leave. She wore a helmet and carried a whip. She has stubborn instincts, Leon thought for no good reason. Perhaps she believed their meeting was one huge mistake, a horrible accident. Leon sighed. Lil would have told him so. She was brave in dismissing him.

Lil's friend, Herbert, shook his mane, yawned at the people drinking and dancing. He didn't see well anymore, couldn't hear the band's gaudy music. His bones surfaced, his skin was patchy. He licked Lil's hand with a large, rough tongue and she stubbed out her cigarette on the ground. His whiskers fanned around his face, blew forward sometimes like thick spider webs. His ears twitched. Lil loved his cushioned muscles and the way they still worked, the warmth of him, his dense, heavy body, his weight thrown back and forth in the music-shattered air, moving on his paws. He could still break a small woman's body in two but the Beckers kept him well fed with raw meat bought fresh from a local butcher. Or else, what would happen? Would it be a bad way to go?

Lil's eyes fixed on Leon sitting in a tall chair, his angular face slack, a rope hung loosely around his neck, his blonde, unkempt hair. She pulled at his rope. Then she dropped the rope and turned away. She could see her mother's bloated face swinging from the ceiling. The pick against his chair was also an unwelcome thought.

"Izzy wanted to wear a sheet and come as someone from the Ku Klux Klan, but she figured not everyone would appreciate it." Her whip unfurled, a snake resting at her feet. "I suppose I should follow the Indians."

"Let's go sit somewhere else for a while. How about outside near the lake?" he asked.

Lil glanced at the lion patiently waiting for her, his paws soft on the floor. That kind of love didn't interest her now, with its obedience. "Have you heard how Giacometti, a new sculptor and painter in Paris, chooses his models? He goes to a whorehouse and chooses the thinnest, sickliest, and syphilitic ones."

"Maybe he's only picking what he already sees in himself or everyone around him," Leon answered too quickly.

"Or there's Picasso who reassembles his women."

"I know," Leon said. "What about George who pretends to think so highly of women?"

The lion circled the floor and lay down, sighed loudly with sour breath. Lil pointed a shoe at Leon. "And what is it that you want from a woman?"

"I don't know yet." Leon couldn't say he wanted someone brave, someone who could see the larger picture.

"We'll have to stand you by an empty canvas, get you a
model, and see what you do with it all."

"Never," he laughed. "I've proved that I'm only good
with numbers."

"We can go outside to the lake. But I have to put Herbert
to bed first. You go on ahead." Lil led the rising Herbert out-
doors where the air had grown crisp and sharp. The laughter
and conversations between people who didn't know each
other's names, and didn't want to, grew to a hush. Herbert
tossed his mane, sniffed at the wind as though it were an
appetizer. His paws lifted gracefully and he moved quietly
into the barn. Lil locked the door; when she turned around
there were two girls standing behind her in the moonlight.

One, a blonde with tinted hair, jumped from leg to leg
as though machine guns were aimed at her feet. She was
dressed in an aquamarine gown with strapped shoes. She
could have been anyone. Her earrings rattled against her
jaws. The other was a brunette dressed as a nurse. Her white
outfit shone in the dark. Her white stockings were wrinkled
and caved in at the knees. Lil couldn't see her hair, it blended with the night, but her lipstick was smeared now, a red
slash reaching across her cheek.

"I know you," the brunette wagged a finger at Lil. "You're
a real live wire."

Lil was skeptical. Women like these two would share
a cheap, city apartment with a fire escape above an alley
littered with broken bottles and other people's trash. They
would forget to water their plants, which would turn into

brown, bent vertebrae. Their windows would become so grimy from cigarette smoke that one girl would tell the other that she was thinking of moving so she could see out a window. The other girl would reply that she had lost a pair of good shoes in her pile of dirty clothes stacked like a large nest at the foot of her unmade bed. She was tired of the other girl's boyfriends coming and going and she was thinking of moving too.

"From where?" Lil asked.

"Maybe the newspaper where I work?" The brunette wavered. She carried whisky, which spilt from its bottle.

"No." Lil thrummed her fingers against the wooden door to the barn.

"I know, I know." The brunette faced her blonde friend and jumped up and down. "From the hospital where I had an appendicitis a few years ago."

"No," Lil said quickly.

"Bellevue hospital. You were at the end, near the window. You were all bloody and gimped up. They said there had been a stabbing but you kept on trying to draw, even in the hospital ward. You told the nurses to bring you paper and a pencil. Then you stuck the paper on a magazine on your knees and drew the hurt people around you. It was balled-up stuff. Then you wanted to try 'collaborative drawing' where you did a part of somebody's body and then passed it on to somebody else. But no one wanted to play that game. People thought you were strange and they said you were stuck on some guy. The nurses watched you and you kept on calling for Henry or George or someone."

"Were the drawings any good?" Lil asked.

"I don't know. You acted like you were left holding the bag." The brunette didn't look at Lil anymore. Her hand was on her friend's shoulder.

Lil held out her hand and the blonde handed her the bottle. She tipped it into her mouth and emptied it as both girls watched. She wiped her mouth with her hand and returned the bottle to the blonde.

"No, I don't know you at all," Lil said and left them standing there.

One girl said to the other, "What's eating her?" as Lil walked back toward the tent pulsing with jazz.

Sgraffito

Alice closed her eyes to the delicate, intricate seeds spilling from a large painted pomegranate. They tumbled out like shiny beans, scattering below the picture edge onto the imagined floor beneath. A white rose hovered over the fruit. A still life offering itself. Her own life hadn't been still. Alice had never placed flowers in a painting before. I'd call her Rose, she thought. Her hair would be the color and sheen of wheat. She would wait for Alice at the grove of gingko trees that lined the park, teeming with other children on swings and playing with balls. Her golden hair would be stitched with sunlight, making it whiter. She would be obedient only with Alice, fussing with everyone else.

"Today," Alice said to George, "I'm in love with lines." She didn't say: not your decision to never have children. She was growing older by the day, giving up so many parts of herself.

"Particularly the sensational ones, I hope," George said in the cramped studio. His mustache twitched as though he was about to sneeze. He wanted a glass of water. He wanted Alice to get it for him as she usually did, but she was painting.

"The indiscreet ones tire me out. They require too much attention." She waved her hand in front of her painting. "Right now, I want subtlety, some kind of loyalty." She

wondered at the awkward gestures between George and
Lil, the spaces, their roving hands. She knew that it had been
over for a while, but she wondered if something had begun
again. She didn't really want to know.

George kept track of Alice's monthly bleeding. He refused to sleep with her at the times he deemed dangerous.
She couldn't win him over or change their agreement. He
had done this with his wife after their daughter was born.

She dipped a palette knife into a deep blood red. She
wanted blood. Earth and water. Rendezvous. Even the
word seemed strange. A rendezvous of flesh, a stranger.
Alice didn't mind the strangers George was interested in
at the gallery. They were soon swept away, involved with
other things or husbands. She wished for a co-conspirator,
an endearment who witnessed everything, George's broken glass, the jarring middle-of-the-night phone calls, bills
from gambling or trinkets she never saw, his starched shirts.
With all the years between them, George sometimes was an
anachronism, a rash that could be scratched too much. He
was handsome and his betrayals were sudden, unplanned
accidents. Alice hadn't ever had the time or inclination. Not
yet. She would have to accept her unsettled stomach, or the
insertion of a tiny insect onto the fruit in her painting, indi-
rect light or the ache of George's mustache along her neck
and shoulders. So far, these had been enough.

George walked by the window in their living room.
Buildings leered at him. A cleaning woman was washing a
window across the street. Big, sudsing bubbles that flowed
down the glass, staining the brick below the sill. An overhead light flicked on and then off in another apartment. Al-

ice wasn't her usual, placid self. Her threadbare, gray sweater had been unraveling and her sleeve hung too close to her paints. He would find her another.

He drank a glass of water in the kitchen. He would go to the gallery. Perhaps Mary would be there. Mary's hair was a diffused red under the lights. She was a good helper, attentive to customers, and she recently began speaking about the textures in art. He overheard her talking of a "smooth" blue picture and a "blistering" clay piece. Where had she learned this? She whispered to him, "I think this woman's a piker." And she was often right.

George's hand rested on the glass. Alice was a genius while these young women were waiting for someone else, someone who was a concert pianist, an industrialist, a gangster, a doctor, their father, anyone more interesting than their husbands. He cleaned and rinsed his glass, not wanting Alice to be distracted with petty tasks. He liked doing things for her at the same time he wanted her to do more things for him.

He stood at the window in the living room, thinking that what he saw was a small part of the width and breadth of New York, a few of its many inhabitants. Soon they would all know Alice's name. She would be mentioned at cocktail parties by heiresses. By the paper boy and the milk man. There was something about the fruit she painted, the way it opened, called out to the viewer, then slapped him in the face. It was modern, like the times.

In the bedroom with its spare furniture, George's small photograph of clouds hung a little askew over the bed. George straightened it.

"I'll dream of pillows and gossamer silk," Alice declared when he had first hung it.

"I hope it'll inspire fucking and crying," George replied.

George rummaged through Alice's sweater drawer in the wooden dresser with a few pale cornflowers painted on its sides. His hand hit the pile of letters he had written to her at the end of his marriage. He ignored them and his fingers passed through pulled yarn, tattered collars, and loose strings. He raised a blue sweater with a flattened collar, one small hole at a shoulder seam. It smelled slightly of turpentine.

He knocked at her studio door and pushed it open, holding up the sweater, but she didn't look back at him because she was in the midst of scraping white brushstrokes from her canvas. He would tell her that he thought the pomegranate could use a little more orange around its edges, a suggestion that she could either take or leave. Metallic gray shimmered from her dark hair.

"Here's a warmer sweater for you, Alice dear. One that shouldn't dip into your paints as much," he told her back. "You could wear it for that *Harper's* article. I forgot to tell you that they called again this morning and said they want to see you tomorrow at two."

"Of course," she said to the litany of fallen seeds, the burgundy fruit, the space where the rose had been.

Thursday 3 pm Session. Notes on the Sublimation Case of Lillian Moore: Patient's hands are crossed. She appears reserved.

Doctor: So let's discuss your mother.

Patient: Then you'll want to know about her crush. He was a real palooka who worked at a grocery store. A younger, mean-spirited sort of man. He always came over before my mother got home from her job.

Doctor: And what did you two do?

Patient: Necking games at first. He thought he was handsome. And then, when I was thirteen…

Doctor: Yes?

Patient: The first time I thought it would stop, but it didn't. He thought I was a pushover. I left my body behind. He did whatever he needed. He told me how he wanted to be a fly boy and yet I was the one that looked out the window at the sky, away from that house. My body grew empty. I tried to live in the clouds, but my mother never noticed. She was a real sap. She was too busy with him, worrying about how she looked and what time he was supposed to show up.

Doctor: Did you ever tell her about him?

Patient: No. My mother was carrying a torch for him. I was what was given up.

Doctor: What happened?

The Patient smiles: He ran off with some dumb Dora one day and didn't tell anybody. A week later my mother hung herself from a light fixture. I found her in our bedroom, her face swollen. Her shoes had fallen off. I couldn't look at her expression.

Doctor: How are you feeling?

Patient: I'm still not sleeping.

Doctor: Can we talk about the stabbing?

Patient: You want everything?

Doctor: Yes.

Patient: It was after the child. Can we talk about it another time?

Case Cause Possibilities: regression. Manifestations: trauma, catharsis, conversion. Symptoms of repression. Use of transference might be effective in this case.

Concerns: Psychosis from prolonged insomnia.

A red dragon lantern swayed above Sherwood Anderson's head as the round, white table, the usual Round Table, was filled with steaming Chinese food.

"I do miss the Midwest with its sweeping cold and snow over the corn fields. The vast emptiness as far as you can see. Look what I have relinquished to live in New York."

Dreiser was already standing up, his head perilously close to the swinging red fringe on the lantern. "Oh, come on, Sherwood, we're late for a drink with that despicable woman, that journalist. I'll help you make your way through the wasteland of Central Park. There should be enough cold out there for you tonight." His suit was in disarray and wrinkled, as though he had borrowed it. A small lump of rice had dried at his knee. Alice brushed it off with her napkin.

"Fine," Sherwood Anderson replied. "I heard that they just elected a female governor in Wyoming." They left, discussing a woman's fitness for office.

"The writers tire me out with their suffering and pretending and the popular revolutions of their politics," Marco said to no one in particular. His tooth gleamed in the pocket of his mouth.

Izzy sat next to him, her hair a dark bouquet. Her dress was embroidered with birds at the neck. She had worn her voice out and didn't want to speak. "This whole era exhausts me, and yet it feels like it's the beginning of so many things to come."

"I'm sure the writers say that we bore them," Lil said. A tongue of meat and round water chestnuts rested in a swirl of noodles on her plate. "But there is more to say."

"I don't know." Alice's cardinal sweater was a size too large. It smelled of cinnamon. Her face was disheveled, her hair slapped her ears. "The writers and the musicians," she nodded to Marco and Izzy, "seem more ethereal to me, creating without a model, plucking their art out of the very air."

"That's not true, Alice. What do you think abstraction is? Abstraction can describe the space around things or the things themselves." Lil twirled a fork in her fingers. "All the arts describe what isn't exactly in front of you."

"Or it can come from a sound or an image that's not really there," Marco added, tea at his lips. He was watching the red carpet, thinking of almond cookies.

"I think jazz depicts the violence done to our hearts," Izzy managed in a little, apologetic voice.

Leon wanted to touch Lil, the landscape of her soft, small body. He thought instead of the carved and inlaid boxes in the glass cabinet near the cashier. How all the individual stones became beautiful next to one another. Each needed the others to create the full effect, to give it meaning. The perfect conjunction of space and time. Jade animals adorned the corners like Chinese cautionary tales, stories of lost children and the animals that saved them. Or the punishing flock of birds, or the dismemberment of a god. The cash register rang as two flappers with predatory long legs paid, pulling out bills from their tiny, beaded handbags. Their voices ricocheted from the red walls.

"My fortune cookie says smackers are coming my way. Can you give me some credit the next time we come in?" She smiled at the man behind the cash register, drummed her fingernails on the counter, and held out her palm.

Her friend added, "Mine said: Don't beat the band, play with it. What do you think that means?" The toe of her shoe scratched her leg.

"I don't know, but it's time to get a wiggle on," her friend answered.

Marco said too loudly, "I love those flappers. They're all nerve."

The flappers left.

George lined up all the fortune cookies. Little, twisted, hard-shelled mouths, in a straight line across the food-soiled tablecloth. He picked the third one in. He cracked it open and read, "Silence becomes you." He roared with laughter. "This one can't be mine." He didn't know what else to say. He didn't say anything more.

Alice's fingers hesitated, then picked up a cookie from the center. "Listen to your dreams. Umm." Cookie crumbs fell on the front of her sweater as she ate. She didn't bother to brush them away.

Izzy whispered, "You long to see the great pyramids in Egypt." She smiled tiredly.

Marco grabbed a cookie and placed it on his empty plate.

"I don't want to know my fortune. At least not yet," he said.

"Go ahead," Lil said to Leon.

Leon broke his and read the thin little paper silently, showing it to Marco, who sat next to him.

"You have to read it out loud," George commanded.

Marco read, "You will meet someone special soon."

Leon blushed. Lil's eyes met his, then shifted away. Leon realized Lil could be thinking anything. She could easily tire of him, find someone else. She might have already.

Lil enjoyed this little drama, theatrically splitting her cookie in two, eating the halves and slowly extracting the paper. Her dark hair fell in her eyes. Her fake startled gesture wasn't intimate or personal, but directed at the table, the room. She hid her eyes behind the tiny paper. Finally her deep voice claimed as she read, "You are going to kill someone who is annoying you."

"Let me see that," George said.

Lil crumpled the paper and tossed it aside.

~

McLaughlin's Cod Liver Oil Tablets

Do you want ambition, energy, and endurance? Tired of being tired? Or bilious? Thanks to medical science there's no more reason to complain.

McLaughlin's Cod Liver Oil Tablets go directly to the cause of the trouble and help you feel better quickly, safely, effectively. Why be miserable? For more get up and go, take McLaughlin's Cod Liver Oil Tablets.

~

Leon was seeing Lil alone. Clouds smothered the tops of the buildings. Windows gawked, surveying the discards of apartment-dweller's lives, piles of cigar bands and abandoned bottles. Bare trees swayed along the sidewalks, stirring as another vehicle slid by. Lil's hair was a dark scarf in the breeze. The museum came into view, squatting along several city blocks.

"This museum is its own planet. It's enormous and completely full of art. I worship this place," Lil smiled as her heels echoed along the damp cement, then up the hill of steps and through the entrance. "And there's not a lot left to worship these days." Leon was quiet and happy, holding her hand.

They passed relics, statues missing limbs, heads. They walked by ancient paintings and pictures, then a blue Picasso, a red and yellow Matisse, a Degas. The corridors snaked on and on and they would stop in front of something, ponder it, silently move on. The Asian pictures and objects were composed of deranged colors, a red that would scare anyone, a blue that turned purple as they moved closer to it, a black that mocked them, made them shudder. Lil explained the implications.

"It's obvious they used that netsuke on a round belt or necklace. See how there's a hollow circle near the dog's tail and how it's worn and yellowed there?"

"Now I see it," Leon said. "So art has some everyday uses?" He laughed, teasing her.

"Never." She stepped closer to a glass case that held three miniature, upended wooden boats with tiny, busy figures roaming along their decks. Her hair shadowed her face.

"Is art some type of surrender?" he asked.

"There's so much to receive from it."

He wasn't sure whether she'd answered his question. "What's it like to be a Bohemian?"

"Terrible and lovely." She turned toward him. "A lion is always a lion. And a raccoon is a raccoon."

Leon and Lil passed marble sculptures under the lingering light, golden, medieval portraits, still lifes, large, metal armor, and even old jewelry worn by sun-struck queens lifetimes ago.

Leon poked his fingers perilously close to a count's nose on a cracked picture. One of the uniformed guards moved closer.

"Art started in caves." Lil plucked a loose thread from Leon's jacket; his features remained patrician, chiseled. "People have always wanted to express their pain and happiness."

They entered a crowded, dull-colored room with placards that described Howard Carter's 1922 expedition and the twenty or thirty men that excavated King Tut's tomb. Their equipment was on display, balanced on piles of sand, with painted pyramids on the walls in the background. The tools were still dirty. Leon thought of his Halloween costume, of its inaccuracies, the pick not long enough, the rope too thick to actually use. He wondered how you could sift through a woman's inaccuracies. Language was paradoxical and yet it could contain a single illuminating instant.

They read about the mummy's curse and how many of the members of the team, including Belgian royalty, British dignitaries and officials, journalists and other experts, had died too young, soon after cracking open and entering the tomb. In 1923, Lord Carnarvon, who had financed the whole expedition, died of pneumonia and blood poisoning. They had broken the sacred seals of the tomb February 17th, so close to his time of death it was frightening. They had not opened the sarcophagus or coffins.

"They are still afraid," Lil said. She thought briefly of Dr.

Duncan. And she hated the rope, any rope.

Lil concentrated instead on the hieroglyphics, layered and cryptic, untranslated. She stared, with her large, dark eyes, at portions of walls shipped from Egypt with faces and figures that seemed to tell stories, cause-and-effect sorts of things.Women with staffs talking to beings with the heads of jackals, men with skirts gazing at disembodied eyes or fish swimming out of the water. She thought if she looked long enough they would come to life, they would share their visions. She would like a pictorial language, the black and violet symbols that showed scribes writing, beautiful women with headdresses and long necks, with their pet cats and dogs, the men hunting. Were they recipes? Stories? A description of their way of life? Metaphors? Description or judgment, the subtle comparisons between different things. Lil could see herself in the hieroglyphics, short, lime-colored and outlined with black: she was painting all night long. George would be there, petting a stray cat. The mummy's curse was suspended, waiting.

Lil stood transfixed by the hieroglyphics as people, most taller than her, drifted by. A man who was holding a little girl's hand stumbled. His hat rolled away, seesawing along the ground, and then it stopped beneath trampling feet. He let go of the girl's little fist. The man's hand shot out as he nearly fell and the girl's chiffon dress flew away from her. Lil rushed to the vulnerable little girl who was clutching the man's pant leg. The man was repositioning the aberrant hat on his head.

"Are you hurt?"

The girl shook her head, hid behind the pants leg.

"Never take any baloney from anyone," she instructed the little girl. Lil stood as tall as she could and stared at the man.

The man rushed the little girl into the crowd.

Leon almost took Lil's arm to guide her away and then he thought again. The scene had made him nervous. Instead, he ushered her farther, saying, "See what Howard Carter said," pointing at a placard and reading: "The tomb was hidden under some of the huts that belonged to the workers."

Lil went peacefully. "I'm that little girl. I'm always that little girl."

Lil moved toward the placard and read with her finger moving beneath it and her lips mumbling inaudibly. "The King wasn't twenty years old. Robbers broke into one of the King's chambers before the excavation party came, but the odd thing was that they hardly took anything." She turned toward Leon. "Do you think they were afraid of the curse?" Was the curse illness or the relief from it?

"Maybe the loot was too heavy."

"Sometimes there's a reason for accidents." Lil was distracted. She looked up at Leon, recovered herself. "Just like in painting. I can make a mistake and sometimes I love it. It's just the right thing and then I use it over and over on purpose in new paintings. Or it becomes a metaphor for something else."

Leon was encouraged by her sudden good cheer and her smile. They arrived at cases of necklaces with gold and colored gems, figurines, small cat statues sitting at attention, fans whose feathers had long ago disintegrated, a golden mask that the king had been buried in. The display stated that these were objects the king was buried with because he was fond of them. Most of them were made of gold.

"This whole show exists because of an act of vandalism," she whispered into his protruding ear.

"A profitable one." But Leon understood the young king's desire to be with objects that outlasted him. It was the comfort of knowing the limitations of things, too difficult a lesson to learn with people.

She was reading. "They weren't afraid at first." Her hair swung and caught at her red lips, a paintbrush's long stroke. "The curse made them think twice." It was a despicable act. It had been a violation. A strand of hair surfaced along her cheek as she confided in him.

Leon brushed the hair from her mouth and it fell behind her ear again. He bent slightly to kiss her and their lips met. People eddied around them. Leon wished Lil had stolen him. Their feet shuffled on the hard floor. When they finished, they found themselves in the last room, a darkened, small chamber with enormous stones against the walls carved with Egyptian sentences. Rocks had been removed from the inner tomb and carted to the museum for the exhibit, propped against the walls. It was so crowded that Leon noticed the vinegar smell of an old woman standing next to him, her off-the-face hat crushed down onto her forehead. He could feel her odor staining his sport shirt, his beige duck trousers.

Lil stood looking at the hieroglyphics again, as though they could speak to her with their strange language, a combination of mathematics and painting. Configurations that confounded Leon. Their meaning seemed unattainable. Lil looked tiny in her ochre crêpe-de-Chine dress. Even with her heeled shoes, she was as small as the king's sealed sarcophagus sitting in the center of the room. People pooled around it, although it was plain except for scenes and words painted on the sides. No jewels or gold were encrusted on its surface, at least not any more. One woman wore an embroidered Egyptian shirt, all squares with a cat poised in its center, and a skirt with false hieroglyphics on it. She barged to the front, her blonde hair shining in waves. She studied the coffin and then left.

Lil and Leon walked outside, where they could breathe again. They realized they had both felt trapped inside, as the king must have felt, confined by death and its myriad interpretations. The New York buildings stood at attention in the autumn glare. Blocks, with their empty trees, widened around them. The clear sky formed a distant horizon, an infinite hat. They could spread out, relax, after those cramped rooms full of the precious possessions of a life, filled with onlookers.

"It makes me want to chart my life on a blue graph." Lil's hoarse voice flew into the bare branches. "I want to see how much painting I can get done."

"Before what?" Leon asked sadly. He remembered his own black, blue, and red numbers and columns. He wanted to kiss her again, but he found himself saying, "Before you stab someone again?" He had his suspicions about the incident she wouldn't talk about. Some lover? Someone who had hurt her? He was frightened, and excited.

Sunlight was symmetrical on her hair. She glanced at

him, breathed deeply. "Yes, that's right. Art, discovery, history make me want to stab someone." She turned away from him.

~

Breton Creates Surrealist Manifesto

The first "Surrealist Manifesto" was recently issued by Andre Breton. This most interesting document defined "two distant realities" combined to make one, which Breton calls a "hypnogogic state." Humor and many references to the Dada movement are contained within the manifesto. Breton defines Surrealism as "Psychic automatism in its pure state," thought expressed through writing or any kind of art not constrained by reason or moral concerns. He believes that any person, artist or not, can live a Surrealistic life. Dreams are particularly important to Surrealists, Breton claims. He cites Dante, Rimbaud, Baudelaire, the Marquis de Sade, Max Ernst, and Paul Eluard as examples of Surrealists. Critics claim the document is full of conflicting, nonconformist, and fascinating ideas, including, "I could spend my whole life prying loose the secrets of the insane," and "It is living and ceasing to live which are imaginary solutions. Existence is elsewhere."

~

When Leon woke in Lil's bed, he saw an outstretched fan

of empty tree branches through her window. Everything was patterns, he decided. Food, financial statements, hieroglyphics, bushes and treetops, equations, the body, time, even relationships. Were they decipherable? He admired a civilization's ability to create another language. He admired much in other people. Lil's scent filled the bed, for she was, amazingly, asleep. The sheets smelled of cigarette smoke, Chinese tea, overripe pears. He peered underneath the covers at Lil's shirt. No new paint freckled it. She hadn't gone into her studio. He was accustomed to the indelible splatters of cobalt blue or aqua over everything. One morning Leon went to work only to discover that one of his Oxford shoes was covered in dark red drops, ants swarming his feet. On another morning the inside of his shirt had a smear of forest green, an illness. He had learned from Lil the difference between a pale green, a blue-green, a forest green, a jade green, and a dark green. Color was a requirement. Leon didn't move, but he searched the floor for signs of a wet paintbrush, a dirty rag, a misplaced jar of turpentine. There was nothing. Usually he fell asleep and Lil didn't. He was careful where he walked in the morning since the amusement of a foot, wet with brown paint, tracing all his steps on the floor, no longer thrilled him or made him laugh.

Lil's face twitched in her sleep, her hair darkly sprawled on a pillow, her full lips spasmed and relaxed, her elbows nestled near Leon's waist. He was close to her upturned nose. A foot gently kicked him. A prophecy? A humiliation? Variations on dreams that Lil never had. Was she an imposter or a heroine? She was fearless in her painting, in her revelations of life and art, but maybe he would have to save

her. A heroine tied to the railroad tracks with the train coming. Only she didn't cry out. The evil perpetrator was long
gone. He looked at her hidden body, her breath shallow and
drifting. She was somewhere without him. A broken ellipse
of morning light stood unmoving in the room like another
person. It leaned on the far wall, watching them.

He had tried asking her again last night, half joking.
"About the stabbing, should I remove all the kitchen knives
or be more careful around you?"

All she said was, "Of course you heard the rumors. It's
what our group lives on."

"You have your obsessions, but you know you're my obsession."

"If I were you, I'd find another obsession." She looked
around the room. "You believe I'm someone else. And most
days I like being someone else."

Lil screamed, untangling herself from sleep and sheets.
She sat up in bed. The scream was loud but short, a piercing
moment. Leon was shocked and tried to hold her and pat
her back. She refused his touch.

"I screamed, didn't I?"

"Yes. What was your dream about?"

"I was in a row of showgirls. I was kicking with all my
heart, but I fell behind, and when I ducked behind a curtain,
a man grabbed me and began to strangle me." Awake, it
sounded silly.

"Ah, the old trying-to-catch-up dream." Leon tried to
sound wise, sitting on the bed in his underclothes. "A sign
of these times."

"What does it mean, oh interpreter of dreams?" Lil

blinked, propped on an elbow over the blanket. She was glad to have had a dream, her very own dream, and, finally, sleep. Even if it did scare her, that subterfuge of night. This was how the rest of the world felt, disturbed but rested.

Leon confessed, "I've dreamt before that I was back at school, sitting at my old desk, but that I didn't have any clothes on. I was naked and embarrassed. Or, once, that someone was chasing me because they believed I had something important, which I couldn't find anywhere."

"You don't need to show off, Mister. This is serious," Lil stated.

Leon explained, "Mine seem to be about frustration or humiliation." He hated to say it. It was not the American way of admiration and sacrifice. He had his accounting practice, an excess of numbers to rely on. Yet sometimes his dreams were about his work. He would dream about rows of numbers that were all wrong or didn't add up or continued off the page. There were clients who wouldn't or couldn't give him information. Or times when his secretary made a mistake, misinterpreted a call or transposed an amount. There was the occasional bootlegger who sauntered into his office, made an arrogant fuss, brought his secretary a trinket, wanting a favor. That was when he had nightmares.

But he hated to admit it.

Thursday, 3 pm Session.

Patient: You'll be so pleased with me, Doctor. I fell asleep and had a dream.

Doctor: You finally slept?

Patient: Yes, Leon spent the night and the next thing I knew I was asleep.

Doctor: That's very good. Now, what did you dream?

Patient: I dreamt that I was back at my old school, which I never finished. I was behind my desk with my ankles crossed like a good girl. The teacher, a pill, was at the blackboard, scratching away with her chalk. She was giving an anatomy lesson and had a woman sketched out on the blackboard with arrows all over her body. Everyone's eyes were fixed on her chalk. But when I looked down at my lap, I realized I was naked. Then I screamed in my dream and, it turns out, in real life too. I think I woke Leon up. But I didn't want him to help me.

Doctor: That may change.

Patient: That was three days ago and I haven't slept again since.

Doctor: I hope we'll change that too. We still have much to discuss.

Patient: Answer me this: why do you always wear a white linen suit, no matter what season it is?

Doctor: I was told that I look best in white linen. Now I don't have to think about what to wear every day. And you'll remember the suit long after you forget me.

Patient appears to be improving with psychiatric help.

Izzy and Marco sat in Lil's worn, four-room apartment where the windows peered down onto a few skeletal trees along the sidewalk. It was so unlike Alice and George's swanky apartment with its grandiose view, conversations with glass and its transcendence, elegance, restraint. Izzy remembered the four of them, Izzy, Marco, George and Alice, clicking their cocktail glasses together. George had offered a toast to "the kind of art that won't take any wooden nickels."

"Why don't you want to do my portrait?" Izzy asked Lil, her fingers wrapped around the bottle of cheap whiskey she and Marco had brought.

"I want a model with a face that hints at tragedy and the body of a saint. I want to show the ruin," Lil stated. She straightened up several copies of movie magazines splattered across her table, *The Tattler* and *Around Town*.

"Izzy has the face of a saint and a tragic body." Marco leaned back into the lumpy green couch; his gold tooth showed. An old, rusty chandelier hung tentatively above them. He held out his glass to Izzy.

Izzy punched him in the shoulder and made a face. "You're never on the up-and-up." She began to pour.

"You wouldn't like me any other way."

"And you wouldn't like me shapeless."

The telephone rang and Lil stood. Her blue shirt had bone-colored abstract mouse marks on the back. Did she back into a wet painting? Marco didn't know how she could get such a strange design. He whispered to Izzy, "I'd like you in any form." He kissed her on the nose as Lil talked in her low, deep voice on the telephone.

"I've heard that George is having financial problems," Izzy said.

"That's nothing new," Marco replied.

"I hope he doesn't lose his gallery." Izzy sipped delicately.

"That would be the last thing he'd let go."

They both heard Lil's voice rise, low and uneven. "That's too permanent, and anyway, it has nothing to do with me." She hung up the receiver and lit a cigarette as she turned back to her guests. "There are too many imposters. There are too many frauds preying on people's fantasies. It's terrible."

They didn't know what she was talking about. Someone trying to sell her something? Leon? George? Marco figured everyone had problems these days. Izzy wondered if the beauty contest had been fixed, like the World Series a few years ago that she had actually bet on.

"Yes, there are," Marco responded agreeably, swishing the liquor in his glass. A splash embroidered his hand and he licked it off.

Lil stood, distracted, and inhaled from her cigarette. When she exhaled, a long wisp of white smoke spun in the air and then rose higher, aiming for the chandelier. Wind pulled a loose paper bag past her window. She stared at the narrow, indented space on the green sofa between Izzy and Marco.

Izzy was about to say something about her set last night, how one of the songs was about a lovelorn woman looking through a fruit vendor's stack of fragrantly sweet oranges for solace. Each one fooled her with its scent. Each one seemed so colorful and delicious. But when she finally decided on one and sliced it open, it was rotten inside.

Marco had walked around Lil and was about to let the needle touch the gramophone record already sitting on her Victrola. He looked at the label first; it was Bessie Smith. He nodded approvingly. "The most interesting person I've met in a long time except for…"

There was a knock at the door and Lil went to open it. She checked her watch first and said, "Oh." Lil flung the door open and said "Hello" to Mary Beach, who entered dressed in black and white, a long string of pearls hanging nearly to her waist. Her red hair was flat against her pale skin. Marco recognized her as the new, married woman from George's gallery. He noticed a broken capillary under the translucent skin at her neck, a few freckles dotting her forehead and a few more in the shape of a lattice across her nose. A little girl with bright red hair, a bow, and a flowered dress followed behind her.

"Izzy, Marco, you won't be wet blankets and say anything to George, will you?" Lil smoked her cigarette as though she could inhale relief. She had no regrets. They nodded their assent. "You both promise? The portrait's a surprise."

"It'll also be a surprise to me," Mary Beach said, cigarette smoke settling on her hair. "She keeps on giving me the bum's rush until it's done." She sat the girl in a chair and told her, "Beatrice, be swell and dry up. Let Lil paint."

"Ah, the sign of a true artist. Silence." Marco helped Izzy stand. "We must leave now." They left with their music and small flirtations.

Lil wanted to talk to someone who didn't use deception, who wasn't overtly cruel, who wasn't too afraid. Mary Beach might do, although Lil couldn't talk about George just yet, with Beatrice there. Lil poured Mary a drink which she politely refused. Then Mary posed trepidatiously.

"Beatrice," Lil told the little girl, "I want to make a happy painting soon. One with a girl just like you. Would you like to pose with your mother?"

Beatrice's red hair flew around her head. "No," she whispered. "It's too scary."

"Maybe after you've seen your mother model for a while. Your hair is beautiful. Now let me know if you get too bored and I'll find something here for you to play with." But the girl was already intently watching Lil with her brushes and paints.

"How did you get that scar?" Lil asked Mary. It was a long, delicate trail carved into Mary's flesh up her leg to below her knee. A wandering white vein on the surface of her alabaster skin. Bird tracks. A new language. Lil wanted to trace it with her fingers.

"My husband," Mary answered.

George hesitated outside the frosted-glass office door etched with "Leon Shaffer, Accountant." He didn't have any partners. Good, thought George. He opened the door to a secretary with pottery bracelets that danced badly on her arm, running into one another constantly. Her eyebrows had been plucked to perfect dashes and her red lips stretched over slightly clenched teeth. She was busy and her lively arms clacked across her desk and typewriter. Her bobbed hair was a riot around her face.

It was the time of Leopold and Loeb, when parents kept their children close and hinted to one another about urban ills, especially in Chicago. New York wasn't immune. Everyone felt they could have been Bobby Franks, the easy victim, taken for a ride and murdered for no reason other than the enactment of the perfect crime.

Shadows washed around George as he smiled. A neparper and an envelope were tucked under his arm. She ignored him from the large, rectangular island of her desk. She shuffled books and papers, answered the telephone, looked at George. To her he was a handsome, older man with a thick, gray mustache, and intense eyes. He was a bit of a rag-a-muffin around the edges but not bad.

"Do you have an appointment?" she asked him across the safe expanse of her desk.

"No, but I'm a friend of Leon's. Of Mr. Shaffer." He smiled again. "My name's George Holman."

"That's what they all say." She extracted a slick, black appointment book, scanned it, and said, "I'm sorry. Mr. Shaffer's busy today. But I could make you an appointment for next week."

George's newspaper dropped onto the floor and as he picked it up he looked at one of the headlines.

Baseball's First Colored World Series Takes Place in Kansas, Missouri

"The newspapers talk about everything but love, but love can't be avoided," George exclaimed.

Alma, the secretary, became alert to him. "Why? What column were you looking at? The free-love sex harems, that one about the gangster's moll, or maybe Houdini, who's a sap for his wife, Bess, and his mother?"

He noticed the drooping tulips on her desk, probably given to her by Leon a few days ago. Leon would forget her and then suddenly remember her, then forget her again. Or maybe they were from someone else, who wasn't thinking about her as much as he should have been. "I was thinking of Leopold and Loeb."

Alma wrinkled up her face as though she had just discovered a dead mouse at her feet. Her eyes refused his, alighting on another piece of paper filled with numbers on her desk. She was about to reach for it.

"No," he said. "Think about it. Who did they commit this perfect crime for? They didn't really want to be caught. Who, then, were they proving something to? And why? It was a secretive act that bound them together, the way all secrets do."

"Umm, I never really thought of it that way." She fiddled with her nails. "I guess so, sure, it could have been love. A balled-up kind of love."

"Isn't love strange?" George smiled and extracted a thin chain necklace with rhinestones and a small, sad blue stone clustered in its center from his pocket. It swung from his fingers. "But you must know all about that."

Her telephone screamed, and her papers trembled at the noise, but Alma ignored it and looked into George's eyes. He placed the necklace on her desk in a small, careless heap. The telephone grew silent, her papers resting quietly again. She looked at George as though she were seeing him for the first time, a gray but appealing sheik, attractive enough. Someone who would share wine, bread, and cheese after a

movie about some gold digger or hoofer who was on the
lam. She fingered the chain on the necklace. Someone who
would kiss her heatedly at her door, polite yet passionate,
older yet young at heart. He would think about her the rest
of the week. She fixed the clasp at the back of her neck. The
blue eye at the center stared at her. Someone who might
come to understand her.

Alma stood and knocked at the door behind her. "George
Holman is here to see you, Mr. Shaffer, if you're not too
busy. He says he's a friend." She was halfway into Mr. Shaffer's office.

Alma turned toward George. "He said you can go in
now." She touched his arm as he passed her. She nodded
at him.

"Hi, Leon." George shut the door, separating them from
Alma. He shook Leon's hand. "Good to see you, old friend."

Leon sat back in his chair, noticing George's discour-
aged mustache, the chiseled chin and jaw, the furrows of
unprofitable worry, a mistake by an unseen sculptor that
rendered his face too haggard and tired, while his eyes were
vivid and excited, searching for an escape. Leon believed
that the man before him didn't appreciate all he had, sweet
Alice garnering attention and applause that she didn't care
about, and Lil who wanted George so badly. Alice's extraordinary painting, with fruit that seemed too real. And beautiful Lil, whom George hardly noticed. She was part of a city
landscape, where actions were diminished and talk was lost
to the wind. Leon didn't hate him for it. It had happened
before Leon arrived. He just couldn't understand this man
who was kind, yet too distracted by his own thoughts and

deeds, his own life. George liked women. George loved the shock of the new. In this way, he was so very American.

"What can I do for you, George?" Leon put all his tabulations aside.

"I owe a lot of money."

"To whom?"

"I can't tell you that."

"Why not?"

"We could both be hurt by these people."

"Did you bring any papers?" Leon held out his palm and George placed his envelope in it. "Let me see what I can do."

PART II

Scumbling

Mrs. Becker whispered into the insolent swirl of Mr. Becker's ear, "Why can't I give a party where there are fistfights, love affairs, gambling, angry exotic women, and men too drunk to rise from the bottom of the coat rack?"

"You have, my dear. Only last week Kitty used a megaphone to try and find her husband." Mr. Becker was mixing a cocktail at the bar in the country house. Some fluid spilled onto the table. Suddenly a splattering appeared on his jacket sleeve. He was losing his touch.

Mrs. Becker glimpsed herself in the smooth bar mirror; she looked sulky and old. She sat in a chair and pulled a knitted sweater around her shoulders. "Did she find him?" Time felt apostolic.

"Unfortunately she did, my dear. In a spare bedroom with that strange little chorus girl that looked so much like a boy. The one who skinned her knees at the lake." He handed her the cocktail, passing it over a silver ashtray with a bird about to fly pinned to its side. "Hair of the dog."

"Hmm, I wonder how she did that," and she laughed. She sipped at her drink, surveying the small room that overlooked the lake. It was the color of peaches but had begun to show beige streaks, as if the room were growing old and tired along with her. She wasn't sure what color to paint it next. Perhaps she'd ask Lil, her artistic consultant, although it was probably a mundane question to her. Light scrubbed the room and her limpid hair became tangible. "But, seriously, we must be careful about that lake. It's large and deep and someone could fall in and drown." People were always trying to avoid the consequences of their actions, Mrs. Becker thought.

"What about people who just want to swim a bit in the summer? Since happiness is our vocation, I'd hate to deny it to someone out of needless worry." Mr. Becker noticed some odd kicking in a shrub outside the window. The gray spasm of a squirrel emerged with a brown nut in its mouth. Then the small apparition ran out of his sight. "Of course, a small fence with a gate couldn't hurt. I'll see to it."

"That's good. We should think about our next party. How about a theme? I do love themes. How about Hollywood? So many people at the Halloween party were dressed as movie stars anyway." It was all dispensation for the too ordinary life they led in between the parties. Mrs. Becker liked returning to their white and silver apartment in New York City when things were too slow in the country. She liked New York where all the buildings were stacked next to each other like so many cakes in a busy bakery. Cars crawled between them and shops were open late with wonderful, supercilious goods to buy.

"I told you about finding my accidental morals, didn't I, dear?"

"Yes, they are totally ridiculous." She smoothed her dress over her knees, feeling the march of time. Mrs. Becker could still dance well and loved to do so. She enjoyed the movement of her limbs, the motion, wind in her hair.

" I told you how I found my morals when I was chasing some ruffian on the street in New York because he had just stolen my wallet. I tripped over an ashcan and there in an alley, scribbled on the wall, was *why are YOU here*? I stopped, grabbed the thief, and then let the young man go. I wanted to be a better person."

"Yes, yes, yes. You've told me many times. It was a good thing that you didn't have much in that particular wallet." Mrs. Becker rolled her eyes, sipped her drink. The lake seemed so visible and near now that most of the trees had lost their leaves. A large, reflecting eye that mirrored the sky. Tree branches were near the expansive window. He was being silly.

"But my new accidental morals are that I'm all for the dinosaurs. After all, they are older than I am. And it would be interesting if we could dress them up. Give them their own party."

Lil sat alone in a movie theatre. Overhead lights glowed along the blue walls, casting odd, blurry shapes resembling stylized flowers. A few people were scattered in the worn velvet seats and the vaudeville stage loomed in front of them. The screen fit snuggly above the stage, eclipsing the entertainers and giving the large room a focus. Pleated curtains fell open. Lil was prepared to study the successful actresses, the way they moved, the context of their gestures, their facial expressions, their reactions. It was another way of seeing her emotions plastered in front of the world.

The lights went down and monochrome black and white

images appeared, the slightly jerking movements of the people, the shades of gray. Before the organ music began Lil had to ask a woman who was chattering, a few seats over, to pipe down. In the story a girl moved to the city, had a sad life. The man she met at a factory didn't tell her about his wife and child. He gave her an armful of lilies and wooed her and won her, then left her. Too late she discovered that she was expecting a child. Lil's heart rose into her throat and she nearly cried, which she hadn't done in ages and hated to admit to doing at all. She checked herself and sighed, decided that she expected more from the woman. Not this silly surrender to events, the coughed-up version of the country girl. Then, strangely enough, Lil's happiness rose from the debris of the film, from the realization that acting wasn't that hard. Perhaps she could do it too. She thought about singing and dancing. Lil watched the actress closely, while smoking a cigarette. The girl ended up meeting someone new, a nice boy. He could sing and dance too. Lil's heart settled down as smoke wafted into her eyes. She didn't like the way the girl believed all the lines from the boy who didn't seem to have any bones in his body. Lil thought she'd rather be painting, but the screen test was next week.

The lights came on again. Lil was sitting cross-legged on the chair, and she unwound her legs. She stubbed out her cigarette, dabbed at her eyes with a handkerchief. They burned from the wayward smoke. She looked around and noticed several other women crying into their handkerchiefs. For a moment she embraced the idea that she would like to make people cry.

~

Ladies, Here is Your Chance
Learn Marcelling Mr. Regan's Way

Mr. Regan's wave is the ONLY wave. You will have to finish with Mr. Regan if you want to be an EXPERT—why waste your time anywhere else? The demand is greater than the supply.

We Teach All Branches of Beauty Culture
Including Permanent Waving and Hair Cutting, Water
Waving and Wig Making
We Have No Failures
Have you had Mr. Regan's latest shingle bob?
In the Belmont Hotel
Park Avenue at 40th Street
MURray Hill 4872

~

"To the nature of art and reputations," George toasted, holding up a glass of champagne toward the window in their apartment.

They lifted their glasses, all yellow and blistering, to their lips, the nearby skyscrapers watching. Marco and Izzy, Leon and Lil, George and Alice all toasted. Lil watched George's face in the window, a mirror, happy as though he was deeply nestled in a woman's warmth. It was the face he had worn just before Lil had asked him to be faithful to her. He was just beginning to see Alice then. Lil had told him, "Alice is a strategy for getting ahead. I'm a more brutal painter and patrons like being able to live another life through my vision. They can pretend to be daring or dangerous."

"Are you disciplined enough?" George had asked her.

"That doesn't always matter."

But George had already begun to turn away. He walked out of Lil's apartment and never returned. Lil had cried and cried, donned gray clothes in her isolation. She thought about seeing gangsters or women or the boy at the five-and-dime, a teenager who limped. His hands shook so badly when he was near her that he spilled half of her sodas on the counter and had to refill them. Lil overheard him whisper to another boy, "She's the prettiest girl I've ever seen. She's the cat's meow." She liked seeing herself in the new department store mirrors, the way she floated between two mirrors, unaware of her height, how perfect her skin was for rouge or powder. She brought Alice once just to see her stutter, her awkward limbs in tattered clothes, her raw eyes, and the confused lines threading her face under the strong lights. Alice's chin was too long, too pointed.

Alice said, "I prefer places that are much slower and have fewer exhibitions." But they both wanted the same things, although in different ways. There was a naked brutality in that and Lil was used to trading cruelties.

Lil decided she would be alone. She tried to convince herself she didn't need some old man, a man that liked women too much. She enjoyed her friends and would not give them up. Neither would George. They had all met at the Chinese Round Table for a long time before and after and during George.

She thought about working new materials like Wedgwood, leather, rhinestones, or Bakelite into her paintings, but she wasn't that kind of artist. She went to the Lost and Found at the Chinese restaurant and pretended to have lost an ivory elephant charm and an umbrella with white cranes along the edges that wouldn't open. "I really missed these," she said, grasping them. Lil looked at the waiter she had seen many times there for his reaction. There was none. "Thank you. I can't live without them."

But George's face didn't change in the window. He looked pleased. His smile didn't untie itself. "Alice and I are finally getting married. We just bought a boat and we're going to live on it out in Long Island." Everyone's glasses touched.

"You've finally finished with your previous marriage, eh, George?" Marco's tooth gleamed. An anchor tattoo briefly showed beneath the sleeve of his silk shirt. His black hair separated into comb marks, all going in the same direction.

"Yes, I'm done with it. Except for my daughter."

Izzy's dark hair was flattened, her eyes large and dark.

She wore a speckled crêpe dress that resembled a quail's egg. Daytime Izzy was more subdued than Nighttime Izzy. "She's grown now. Isn't she?"

"If you want to call it that." George was still smiling. The afternoon moved around him as though he were in the way.

"Congratulations," Leon said. He was the only person who wasn't surprised. He and George had discussed the marriage because of its financial repercussions. Leon now knew George's life intimately. The numbers molded future decisions and told him all he needed to know about the past, where, when, and how much.

Lil perched on the arm of the brown sofa. A penny fell from her tiny pocket and landed heads up as though someone had flipped it. She sipped her champagne. Her neck grew redder. She had been told this was a simple get-together before they all went out for dinner. The afternoon offered her something else. White walls weren't kind. The floor mumbled. Her face bubbled in the circle of her glass, little explosions that burst at her forehead, cheeks, nose, and eyes. Everyone seemed to be looking at her. She took Leon's hand and kissed it pointedly. Leon smiled. Out the window, the stream of traffic reminded her of paints washing down a drain. "It's not very Bohemian of you," Lil whispered.

"I think I'm forgetting something," Alice said uncomfortably.

"There's only so much anyone can be expected to know," Lil said.

On the way to the restaurant in the cab, Lil took Leon's soft hand again and said, "Let's forget the restaurant and go to my place instead. We can order takeout Chinese food."

Leon kissed her rough fingers, her clavicle. It would all work out. He glimpsed the mackerel-colored sky following the car.

At her apartment they ate quickly and then the rain began outside. Lil's hair flew from her head as she pulled all her clothes off and jumped onto the bed. Leon didn't have a chance to slowly undo her buttons, slipping his fingers between cloth and skin to compare the textures. She traced her fingers along his body, brushing the hair on his chest downward and then the hair on his legs the opposite way. She nuzzled the dip between his neck and shoulder. She refashioned his mouth, stitched his skin with her fingernails. She was silent, never uttered a word.She was painting him, concentrating on the brushstrokes. She tasted of cigarettes, champagne, and Chinese wontons.He reached for his wallet, prepared now. Their hips touched. Their bodies grew and shrank. Her flesh strangled and then released him. They intertwined until each cried out suddenly and then she leaped away from him.

"I can't have children. You don't have to worry," she said. She donned her pale blue robe with its dangling sash, threw on her ostrich feather boa and sashayed toward her studio.

"That's fine," Leon uttered, thinking that sometimes she was a child.

She left the studio door open, which she rarely did, and took a clean knife and cut the unfinished portrait of Mary Beach among the bougainvillea into large, ragged pieces. The ripping noise and the action of her arms made Leon uncomfortable.

She emerged when she was done. "I'll do another one of her, hopefully with her daughter." She brushed her hands together, as though she were finished.

"What happened to you? What about the rumors?" Leon asked. Her eyes were flashing and he thought of the knife.

"I couldn't hurt a fly. At least not intentionally," she said, "but I get angry at myself. Why don't the people I let inside of me want to stay?"

"But that's exactly where I want to be," Leon answered, predictably.

Most nights she was in her studio and Leon read the newspaper until he fell asleep. That night she went into her yellow kitchen, where she unearthed a favorite orange cup and three plates. She was uncharacteristically noisy, insouciant. Leon stood in front of the kitchen cutlery drawers, his body holding them closed. He watched as she threw the china one by one at the floor. "I prefer harder surfaces with better colors and more resiliency."

She reached for more plates.

Leon jumped to Lil's side. He slapped her cheek, gently. She turned her face away from him. He held her arms down and she whimpered a little. When she was still, he began to clean up. Neighbors came by and knocked at the door, but Leon and Lil ignored them.

"When did Alice say they were going to get married?"

"Tomorrow," Leon stated, "at the courthouse. There will be the usual party afterwards at the Beckers."

"Of course." Lil wondered what would really change.

Leon wished he could glue the beautiful dishes back

together, although Lil didn't really seem to care. He swept them into the garbage, where they clattered to the bottom. "I don't know why you stay with me," she said.

Lil thought she heard Izzy singing as she approached Dr. Duncan's office, and she wondered what Izzy was doing in his office. Once she entered the room, she realized that the singing had come from the Victrola. The black, corrugated disk circled around the heavy steel needle perched above the record, caressing it gently. The needle bounced slightly, moving round and round to the center. But the voice slipped into Lil's clothes, agitating her, and making her sad. Dr. Duncan, in his white linen suit with an ochre shirt and a dark tie, removed the needle, and the sudden silence disturbed Lil even more, as if music would no longer return.

"Ethel Waters," Dr. Duncan explained. "Sometimes I play her between patients."

For the first time Lil wondered about Dr. Duncan's personal life. What made him want to listen to people's problems day in and day out? She could barely tolerate her own. What about his loneliness?

"I want to join the circus," Lil began. She lay on the gray velvet couch. The ivy plant was twining near her shoes. She laughed.

Dr. Duncan examined her new outfit, the gold shaggy top with beads over a red skirt. Was she trying to say something? Her gold fingernails brushed aside his ivy to make room for her buckled shoes. An advertisement. The pencil tapping began.

"I'm becoming demented," she offered. She wanted to

scream at him: You're asking me to sacrifice too much of myself to you!

"Isn't all of America demented right now?" Maybe her outfit provoked him. Some days he wanted everything to quiet down. He could put a blanket over her. Save her. There was such a frenzy to everything.

"I'm just talking."

"Have you been sleeping?"

The eternal question. "No. But I'm starting a new painting."

He had hoped the disclosure about her mother hanging herself would allow her to sleep. She fidgeted and he remarked on this in his notes. He needed to go further.

She could see him writing and liked it when he wrote down what she said or did because then she knew it was important. "What do you do with shame and loss?"

"What kind of shame and loss?" he asked.

Lil looked out his window. She wanted to teeter on the edge, jump toward beckoning shadows. She picked at a fingernail and sprinkled gold flecks onto her shirt. "I suppose you can either expose it, lie about it, or let it fester." She was speaking to herself. Lil removed her cigarette holder and a cigarette from her bag and lit the faraway end. Smoke meandered around her prone figure and the scumbled gray velvet.

"Continue."

"My mother wanted to die. She tried hard to accomplish it. She brought home potions to make him love her. She lined up bottles in front of a photograph of him. She tried remedies for all kinds of imaginary illnesses. Some made

her truly sick. Then she started a shrine with one of his ties.
She'd put bits of his hair and threads from his clothes all
around it. She'd pray. She forgot about me and she forgot
about herself." I'm not so different, she thought, but I won't
make the same mistakes. "But she had already lost him."

A pigeon alighted at the window, pranced back and
forth with its sooty feathers. Clouds swarmed behind it. Its
head bobbed. The bird's feet were a nervous sort of house-
keeping.

"How did you feel about him?"

"He was a body. A body that wanted more than he had.
He wanted a caper. I was an unwilling part of the drama, of
the vaudeville show." She smiled to herself. The cold pigeon
watched them for a moment. Lil brushed her gold shirt and
thought of coins. "What do you think of drama, Doctor?"

"It has its place."

"Each body must give permission though. Each has its
own instructions." She lifted her cigarette to her mouth,
tapped the ashes into a round, silver ashtray with modern,
geometric lines that crisscrossed. The ashes buried the design. The pigeon flew off, its wings brushing the window.
"My mother was sad and wrong. But, in a way, she wasn't
that far off center. You can't pick who you love. You con-
centrate on them and go for it. It's just that she forgot about
everything else, including her child."

"And what about him?"

"He shouldn't have done what he did. I've heard that he
manufactures belt buckles in the West now and has a wife
and three children."

"And your father?"

"He was long gone. But I often thought of visiting the Belt Buckle King and watching his face as he realizes who I am, grown up."

"Forgiveness," Dr. Duncan pronounced, as if it were a sacred word.

"But how can you forgive yourself?" She gathered her dangling bag, stubbed out her cigarette. Her shoes appeared solid and sturdy beneath her.

~

Leopold and Loeb's "Thrill Killing" Confessions and Trial

Two university students, sons of wealthy Chicago families, Nathan Leopold and Richard Loeb, confessed to the kidnapping and murder of 14-year-old Robert Franks, who was a cousin of Loeb. The two kidnapped Franks at 5:30 o'clock in the afternoon on May 21, 1924 near his home "in a spirit of adventure" and as the first act in an intended series of similar crimes. It was reported that Leopold stifled the victim with his hand over the boy's mouth and hit him on the head with a steel chisel until the Franks boy was dead.

At 9:30 that evening Leopold and Loeb threw acid on their deceased victim's face, removed his clothes, and placed the boy's body in a swamp. Then they cleaned themselves, played a game of "casino," and went to sleep.

They had begun planning "the perfect crime" more

than six months previously. They had readied a ransom letter but by chance they ran into the Franks boy, so committed the murder sooner than they had planned. They mailed their ransom letter to Mr. Franks and were confident that they would not be caught, but their alibis were discredited and, when cornered by the police, they both cracked.

After the Franks boy's body was discovered by a passerby, a pair of spectacles was found near the site that were traced back to Leopold. The police also obtained samples from Leopold's portable Remington that matched the type on the ransom letter. This evidence helped elicit the two's confessions.

The trial, presided over by Judge John Caverly, has lasted several months so far, with a general outcry by the public favoring execution.

~

"Did you hear that the judge might free Leopold and Loeb?" Mary Beach said, wrinkling her freckled nose, a horizontal woman draped in white satin, a shimmering, moonlit boulevard. Lil rearranged her legs.

Mary's body dissembled into so many different versions of itself. A blue piece of fabric flocked behind Mary's prone figure. Lamplight interrogated Mary's face. Her red hair fell around her neck. "Never. Robert Frank's family will make sure they don't get off. I think people realize that it could have easily been their child that the two boys kidnapped and killed for no reason." Lil positioned Mary's hands limp-

ly at her lap so she resembled someone who had been strangled. She stepped back and looked at the tableau.

"They had to have some kind of a reason." Mary Beach
wanted to scratch her nose, but she knew she wasn't allowed. "In business, like in my husband's business, there's
always a reason, and it's always about the dough."

"Hold still," Lil barked. She was thinking of a body in
white. She wanted to paint differently, move into another
style, as though she could describe the various stages of her
own life, her shifts in thinking or believing. She picked up
a shade of russet on her brush and began an underpainting,
all gauzy lines and shading. But where to begin? To describe
Mary to George, for he was always there between them, unseen.

"George told me that I was on the trolley about the paintings at the gallery, but he called my face 'evasive'." Mary
wanted to talk about necking with him in the back room,
the way his mustache scratched her cheeks, but Beatrice was
in the next room playing with paper and a pencil. Besides,
someone had come through the gallery, and they separated
and grew busy. Mary was glad he was going to marry. She
liked Alice too, although Alice wanted the world to be like
her, quiet and limited.

"George hasn't looked at your face closely." Lil laughed
quietly to herself. If it had been Alice painting her, Mary
would have resembled the membranous segment of a large
pale grapefruit. Lil was adding color, glazing, using her
knife with chestnut, olive, melon-green, pumpkin, pista-
chio. Food colors. Her brushstrokes came quickly. It would
be a change of style. A freedom, if such a thing were still

possible.

Beatrice bounded into the room, her red hair wispy and flying every which way like fur. She had found a fistful of crackers, which she was nibbling, and proudly held out her papers toward Lil with her other hand.

Mary sprung up and her white dress pooled around her. She reached for Beatrice, who said to Lil, "Here, a present."

Mary said, "Baby Doll, mind your potatoes. Lil's busy."

But Lil put aside her own paints and held up Beatrice's stick figures in stick houses. "These are simply beautiful, Beatrice. Maybe you'll become an artist too."

Beatrice giggled and Lil was able to kiss the girl's flimsy hair that smelled of berries and candy. Lil wanted to hold her forever, but Mary took the girl's hand. Lil patted down Beatrice's tremendously red hair before the mother and child went into the next room to leave.

"I've never done this before," George said, the wrinkles at his brow growing deeper.

"Leave it up to me, old sport. We'll figure out how best to celebrate your upcoming marriage," Mr. Becker said, wearing an expensive suit. He brought out several bottles and lined them up on the French table.

The Beckers' New York apartment was at the top floor of a tall, thin, brick building. The walls and floors were white and the furniture carved and ornate. Leon reached for a glass and his hand brushed the head of a painted angel along the table legs. His own legs shivered. He knew he couldn't help George out of his debt and he would have to tell him. Leon had gone over the papers carefully, suspecting Lil was in there somewhere, seeing what George did for Alice as well as for himself. He had bought blue lapis lazuli earrings. For whom? Alice, Mary, Lil, Alma, or someone else? Leon had the facts. He just didn't know what they meant. Leon tried to contact the man who had loaned George money and he had been unsuccessful. A gruff man answered the telephone. "I'll leave him the message. He'll get back to you." The man sounded as though he was picking his teeth.

"I've never been to this kind of party before." Leon looked out the window, but it faced the back of an office building, and all he could see were several empty offices that looked like his own.

"It's not different from any other party. Except that it's all men." Marco was thumbing through pictures in a *Vanity Fair* magazine that he had found underneath a sculpture of a woman in a flowing gown on a table.

George began inspecting the Beckers' paintings. He shuffled from wall to wall, saying nothing. He stopped in front of a photograph that he had taken of Audrey years ago. Audrey was a watercolor painter (not a good one) that George had met at a gallery show. She was not demanding, attractive enough, and liked balancing objects, like wine glasses and paintbrushes, on her nose. Audrey was wedged among round stones, a stone herself, with water flowing over everything. A full moon stared back at the observer. George remembered how the gestures of water mimicked Audrey's own movements, her hands and legs as they wrapped around him later on. They had become part of a gentle current. Alice had been waiting for them back at the house. Dinner was ready. They ran inside, laughing, shaking water everywhere. Would marriage change anything? George didn't believe so. It was better for his taxes and his claims on Alice's painting commissions. He focused on Audrey's cheekbones in the photograph and murmured, "You made me laugh." She was married now and living in another country.

Mr. Becker lowered a needle onto a record and ragtime music began. "Perhaps I need to invite a woman or two. What do you think?" A bowtie hung open at his neck. He was pouring himself another drink.

"Maybe," Leon said, wishing for distractions from thinking about Lil.

"Who?" Marco wondered if he knew the women.

"I could ask my neighbors, Mrs. Mowers or Miss Bishop. All jolly sorts. Or I could call someone if you wished." Mr. Becker filled all their glasses, hit his rim on the one he offered to Leon.

"No," George said, his brows knitting as he stood before a composition made entirely of black, red, and blue lines intersecting one another on a white background. He couldn't remember if he had sold it to the Beckers. It was very modern. "I'm tired of women."

At first Alice considered the dessert fruit bowl picturesque, rather copacetic. Then she decided it was actually less than that, plain and rather ordinary. Couldn't this excellent restaurant think of some imaginative way to show fruit? Something that would inspire her, not merely apples jumbled with pears and a few sprigs of grapes on the top. Oranges, quince, blueberries, strawberries, and bananas, and all kinds of exotic fruit were just waiting for an astonishing arrangement. I suppose I have to show everyone what they're missing, what they don't see, she thought. At least the lunch was lovely. Fish, potatoes, creamed corn. Still she had been hoping for another perspective, at least an interesting mix of colors and shapes.

Lil lifted a piece of chocolate cake to her lips. "To many more paintings."

Mrs. Becker tapped her spoon on her water glass and held it aloft. "To Alice and George. May your marriage be as happy as mine." Her lipstick was awry but her dress suit fit perfectly. "Perhaps we can drink something a bit stronger later on," she whispered to Lil.

Izzy, Alice, Lil, and Mrs. Becker sipped at their water, contemplated their desserts.

"Let me tell you about the sounds of late autumn." Izzy was leaning back in her chair, believing she felt the stares of waiters and patrons alike although no one noticed anything different about her or looked at her. She wore a white dress that tufted around her neck. "The rhythm of rain, the staccato blast of a car, footsteps on wet pavement, the swish of coats and hats. It's all jazz." She lifted her coffee cup. "I hope your marriage will be all jazz, Alice."

But Alice was preoccupied with the fruit that people were hesitant to eat. She took it out of the bowl and arranged it in a circle around her plate. Then she placed each piece back in the bowl. She did this several times. She scratched her chin. She was dressed in brown muslin, her hair pulled back severely. A shredding sweater was draped unbuttoned on the back of her chair. "George said we'll be economizing. We'll be living on a cabin boat vaguely converted to a houseboat." The oranges and apples were in a pyramid that she slowly disassembled, returning each piece of fruit to the bowl. She smiled and it was as though she had just viewed a masterpiece, had escaped from a crowd of cynics and joined a group of fellow believers. A disarming smile.

Mrs. Becker turned to Lil, "How is your work going, dear?"

"Fine." She knew Mrs. Becker wasn't interested in either details or problems about her work. "How's Herbert, my favorite guy?"

"He's fine for his age. He's been bellowing a bit too loudly lately, probably missing you." She tugged at her expensive scarf, decorated with pink birds in various positions of flight.

Later, after George and Alice's simple civil ceremony at City Hall, everyone arrived at the Beckers' country house. Alice had worn a makeshift veil, an aunt's lace curtains quickly sewn into a bridal veil. She wore a bone-colored dress, layered, which she had discovered at a pawnshop.

"It makes the whole ceremony feel more accidental, like finding treasure in a junk pile," Alice said. Her dark hair was buried beneath her veil.

George wore a suit and his mustache was trimmed neatly. He made strange, comedic faces, even during the ceremony. He glanced hurriedly and often at Leon, as though for confirmation and support. Leon nodded and thought that sometimes we fall in love with what someone could do or inspire us to do, not who they are. Like falling in love with weather, or a season, you had to wait and see what they would bring.

Lil stood by Leon's side, her dress a blotchy burgundy. He wanted to kiss her into a bright redness, taste sienna, her arms fidgeting. She said she wanted a cigarette badly. She fingered her handbag. Leon decided that with some women, all a man could think about was redemption and the promise of prophecy. He would wait.

At the Beckers', Lil thought it resembled a circus or a costume party again. Tents reached down nearly to the lake, the glint of jewelry, night flowers nestled among the food and drinks, music and roars of laughter. Some of the ossified people had removed their shoes by the time Lil and Leon arrived. She turned and kissed Leon, his face smooth under his lion-colored hair. Cold rain and raspberries. Lil was afraid the rivers would flood and Herbert, who was resting, would need to learn quickly how to swim.

Outside, their feet sank into the spongy soil. Lil opened her mouth, swallowed rain. She imagined a deep well filling up inside of her, an approximation of being full, yet never overflowing. "So is marriage baloney?" she asked Leon, her mouth wet, glistening.

"It certainly isn't what it used to be." He moved his hand to the small of her back. "For some people it means nothing, to others it means everything. For some people it's just the conclusion of a deal."

"I hope to transcend marriage." Lil moved her arms into

the air as though she were going to fly. "Although I still love
love. Doesn't everybody?"

Inside a tent Leon touched the crown of his hat, removed
the hat, set it aside like a present. "I liked the story I once
heard about a shoe polish industrialist who married a shoe
heiress."

Marco ran up to them with Izzy in tow, smiling his gold-
toothed smile. "Beware of Baby Chapman. She's on her way
here. You two might want to hide." They disappeared into
an adjacent tent.

Lil and Leon looked at one another, Leon peering down
at her. Neither had heard of Baby Chapman. Alice and
George were nowhere to be seen, vanished into the terri-
tory of lifted glasses, dancing, and loud introductions.
They couldn't help overhearing a toothpaste manufacturer
talking to a woman who seemed too scrooched and tired to
answer him. She pressed herself against the wall because he
was so close to her. She was slim and sunburned and was
dressed in white with white flowers that dangled from her
dark hair.

"I've seen the pyramids and tombs in Egypt. I've seen
the real thing in its native place, not all this funny business
displayed in the theatre and museums." The toothpaste
manufacturer puffed on a cigar. A bird flitted into the tent,
skimmed along the ceiling and left again. The man's sturdy, rotund limbs could have easily crushed several wom-
en by mistake. The woman, on the other hand, withdrew
even further against the wall, as if that was all that kept her
from running away. "I like your smile. You have good teeth.
Would you like to come with me on my next trip to Egypt?"

He edged toward her, but she didn't respond except to crouch away from him. Two white flowers from her hair fell onto the floor.

He took her arm. "C'mon. How about tomorrow? There's a ship leaving in the morning. What do you say?" But she twisted her arm away from him and scurried off. The toothpaste manufacturer's eyes stared blankly at where the woman had been. His eyes were blue and unfocussed through the clear glass of his raised drink.

"At least he's not a bourgeois hypocrite," Lil whispered to Leon, "pretending to want something else and then surprising her later on."

"Do you think the Beckers are bourgeois hypocrites?"

"I don't know what the Beckers want. Maybe to be part of something. They seem like good eggs. But they aren't socialists either." Lil lit her cigarette. "I do miss Herbert." She turned and looked up, toward Leon. She could hear a band playing somewhere in the distance. She wondered whether Izzy and Marco would join the band, have some fun with it, or discuss the band's weak points among themselves. The phrase "to beat the band" echoed in her head again and again. That's what she got for not sleeping. Bleary repetitions. "I like to imagine Herbert revived at MGM or at the front of the public library, roaring, of course."

Lil and Leon moved through the chorus of dancing arms and legs, trying not to be targets, and sat down on two chairs that weren't too sticky. The music was too loud to allow talking. Lil's cigarette smoke rose to the tent's diaphanous ceiling, a remade life, porous and insubstantial. It spread out, became invisible, transformed into something else. She thought: That's what new money does. She knew that she wouldn't have minded some of it herself.

A woman who was collapsed or sleeping near Lil woke up, turned to Lil and said, "Do you think I need a new toaster?" The woman's glittering headdress had slipped to the side of her head. She looked angelic and deranged. Everyone was a Bohemian.

The incoming air in the tents was cold and damp. The smell of Lil's cigarettes obliterated the smell of food and hooch. Someone whimpered somewhere. Someone sang, "tea for two, and two for tea." Off key and too loudly. Lil believed she glimpsed Mary Beach's red hair against a man's wide lapel. His hand caressed her bright hair, a gold ring circling the fourth finger of his left hand. A bulge, the shape and size of a gun, bit into Mary's side. He stroked her hair to the beat of the music, as though his attention was elsewhere. Mary closed her eyes, the rhythm of the music the same as his touch. When Lil looked again, they were gone. Lil thought she should add purple, the color of bruises, and a blue-green, the color of an ocean, to Mary's portrait. And red, the color of a wound.

A screeching voice, full of laughter, made its way down the length of their tent. Neither Lil nor Leon could see where it issued from because there were too many people in the room. Then the voice emerged and Leon saw that the older woman coming toward them wore a hat with several small apples and a banana attached to its brim. She had a necklace of empty fruit cans that moved against her chest as she walked. If you could call it a necklace. She sort of swooped about, going from side to side, rattling, as all the

guests made way for her. She seemed cheerful enough. She
stopped short in front of Lil and Leon.

"I don't know you two." She held out her hand and the
cans clattered.

Leon shook it. "You must be Baby Chapman. I'm Leon
Shaffer and this is Lillian Moore."

"Ah yes, I've heard of Lillian." She looked them both
up and down. Lillian was beautiful and her stiff, splattered
maroon dress displayed some new concepts. A good start,
as Baby Chapman perceived it. She'd heard gossip about
her, something about a stabbing and a child, but she wasn't
sure who was stabbed and whose child it was. The man was
pleasant-looking with thick, blonde hair, but he showed no
initiative and such a plain suit could be seen anywhere, at
restaurant counters, on the streets, on lawyers and bankers.
"Do you like my tribute to Alice's work?" She bent down
and displayed her hat, fingered a can with a label depicting
plums, huge and ripe and still hanging in a grove. "The fruit
she paints is so sexual, don't you think?" As she shivered,
the cans clapped. But she didn't wait, "Adventure beckons."
She moved noisily on, an entourage of people following in
her footsteps.

"At least she wasn't dressed as one of George's nudes,"
Lil said, her voice deeper than usual. "Let's go out and get
some air," she suggested. Baby's display required either a
shedding or an assertion of one's identity.

Cooler air swirled around them. There was a rush of
noise like leaves cackling. But it was much quieter outside
than at the party, than in the tents with their music and the
wet voices. It was dark outside. The faint moonlight that

coated the trees scattered itself over water. Lil held his arm as they drifted toward the lake.

"I wonder if people are products of their age. I mean, if Baby Chapman didn't exist, would we have to invent her?" Lil looked up at Leon's vanishing and reappearing face. "If someone had to make her up, I'd hope that her wardrobe would be better." The nuances of black slowly became gray as her eyes grew accustomed to the dim light.

Leon turned downwards, toward her. "What would America be without its artists and accountants?"

They were at the edge of the lake. The rain had stopped. It felt mythical. The calm eye of the moon stared at them from the water, stars pulled themselves upward, mills and towns blinked in the distance. There were the quiet, open mouth of water, the stones at their feet, and the skeletal trees. He watched Lil's profile as she looked at the water. Leon could feel her spine in his palm, his hand around her waist. His feet sank if he stayed in one spot too long. Soon they would be the same height. There was a rustling, a nervousness among the trees.

"Memory never helps," she answered absently, as though she were having a completely different conversation. As he bent down to kiss her she pointed at something at the edge of the lake. Leon looked up, slightly annoyed at the distraction, and saw something, maybe a figure with a dash of pure white, which seesawed at the edge of the lake, fell, and then splashed in the water. The night grew silent again.

Leon and Lil walked over to where the noise had been. Lil wondered if it was some kind of a dream. An animal, Leon deduced, one that liked water and hadn't surfaced yet.

Then they picked up two white flowers and at the same time recognized them, just as an arm reached out of the lake. A woman's head was visible with dark, wet hair. She struggled and splashed. The moon's reflection disappeared.

Lil looked at Leon and touched the water with one toe of her shoe, tentatively, "I can't swim." Her raucous voice skidded. She slowly removed her shoes.

"No, I'm a strong swimmer." Leon was already at the edge of the lake.

The woman who had slunk away from the toothpaste manufacturer waved her arms, her mouth open, but she didn't say anything. The splashing seemed to go on forever. Leon threw off his shoes, his jacket, his trousers, and Lil picked them up and held them as though she were about to arrange a still life. Leon dove into the water.

Lil yelled toward the direction of the party, "Help us out here. A woman is drowning. Help." She didn't know if anyone could hear her, so she ran back toward the Beckers' house.

The woman's head sank below the water and sky. Stars looked on, blinking yet recognizing their limitations. It was frightening but it didn't seem quite real. The water rose slightly, in small waves, as Leon swam quickly toward the middle. He dove underneath where he had last seen the woman's arm. He surfaced and looked around at the glassy sheet, and then dove down again. Up came two heads this time. The woman's head was tilted and there were no more flowers in the hair plastered to her head. Their faces dissolved against the night water.

Leon was glad that the woman had stopped flailing.

When he swam underneath the second time to find her, she was floating with her clothes spread out, a white flag waving in surrender. He held her thin body, she felt weightless. He grabbed her and lifted her head. The chill water had raised goose bumps all over his arms and legs. He was so cold it felt as though he were encased in ice, especially since he wasn't swimming as excitedly anymore. He pulled the woman's limp body along with him and the cold penetrated his skin. He withdrew deeper into himself, to a warm core, his outer body slow, thick, frozen.

Leon whispered, "Are you there? Can you hear me? Tell me your name." A strand of her dark hair was lashed to her cheek. She didn't respond. He could feel that his legs were still moving, avoiding her drifting ones that seemed to constantly get in the way. He held her at her waist, where he had held Lil a few minutes ago. Her arms and dress were floating on the surface. He couldn't wait to get out of the freezing water so he kicked, although he felt soft things surrounding his legs, maybe fish or algae, moss creeping from rocks.

As he neared the shore with his cargo, Leon noticed that a few people had gathered there with Lil. In the dark, Herbert's pair of yellow eyes. George, Mrs. Becker, and three people he didn't know were waiting. He started out of the lake, but the cold fingers of water gripped him like mud. People ran to his side and carried the inert figure of the woman. A man he didn't know began beating her chest, breathing in her mouth. "A doctor," someone said. Some of the lake water spouted from her mouth, and the woman gasped for breath. She was alive. Good, he thought. Someone wrapped Leon in a towel, but his limbs still shook and cold water ran down his back and stomach.

"I thought we might both disappear." Leon's teeth were chattering. It wasn't quite what he had meant to say. In the cold water the human body wasn't as buoyant as he thought. Thank God it wasn't an ocean with currents. The woman was alive. He inhaled the cold night sky and a chill ran through every little vertebrae, every rivulet of his skeleton.

"Let's get you to the house and changed," Lil said. Herbert trotted slowly along behind them, eyes glowing in the dark.

A woman he didn't know with blonde, wavy hair stopped them, patted Leon on the back and said, "You're a real hero."

Inside the house Leon and Lil hurried upstairs. Everyone made way for Leon, who was dripping all over the floors, and some partygoers patted him on the shoulders and said things like, "Good job," or "Attaboy, you saved her life!"

Herbert stayed downstairs, too old to climb. In a bedroom Leon shivered as Lil changed him, giving him a pair of Mr. Becker's socks and one of his shirts. She held out a pair of Mr. Becker's white boxer shorts. Leon shook his head, his darkened, wet hair flying, and pulled on his trousers, which had a streak of dry mud near a pocket. They could hear the faint cries of an ambulance and the police growing closer.

"They'll want to see you," Lil said.

"I'm exhausted," he said to Lil. "I'm going to find someone to drive me home so I can sleep. I'll call you." He looked at her liquid eyes and hurried out of the room, down the stairs, past many of the guests who had already resumed their party. He knew what had happened but he wasn't sure who it had happened to.

Imprimatura

There were photographs of a startled Leon on all the front pages of the newspapers.

Hero Saves Woman from Drowning

Two reporters from smaller, local papers had arrived at the Beckers' house and clicked the pictures as Leon hopped into some partygoer's car to go home. He had been surprised. His wet hair was plastered onto his head, his eyes were large and flew off the page past the edges of the photograph. Reporters had lined up to shake Leon's hand while an older man, a Mr. Henry Drake, was patiently waiting at the steering wheel. "You're a hero, son. Of course I'll give you a ride back to the city," Mr. Drake exclaimed. Leon had asked the first person he saw at the Becker's party.

An ambulance had taken the woman, whom no one, including the Beckers, seemed to know, to the hospital where the attendants said that she was going to be fine. Leon barely remembered her tan, lithe body, the crushed white flowers in her dark hair, her white, skittish dress, and the shoes she lost, probably in the lake. She had seemed scared already, the first time he had seen her at the party, frightened and running away. More could have happened at the lake.

Then larger papers in New York picked up the story,

ran the same picture. They wanted an uplifting story, something besides Leopold and Loeb or gangsters. Leon sat in his office receiving telephone calls; most expressed their awe of his spirit, several scolded him, wanting to complain about their lives to somebody, and one anonymous caller said, "You should have let that dame drown. I would have."

What had the woman been trying to do?

Alma had taken to wearing more make-up, waiting for reporters to ask her something about the story and what she knew. Her new face powder misted his accounting documents, turning them shades of beige. Her magenta mouth formed new shapes, deciphering the various callers. She'd yell, "This one's an earful but okay," or "I'd tell this one to scram" but he always talked to them anyway. He hadn't had a chance to do much work in the last week. So this was what it was like to be a hero, even an accidental one, Leon thought. He didn't have any aplomb like Lil, only instinct. Luckily he had learned to swim during his Midwestern boyhood. Anyone would have done what he did. His life had become a fabricated life in the newspapers, one that even he no longer recognized. He didn't really like all this adoration and he wasn't sure Lil would. It was an abrupt action with its own consequences. He didn't know how to get out of its way. He thought again: Beware whom you admire. All he wanted to do was to see Lil, whom he hadn't heard from for at least a week. He already knew that love couldn't save anyone and it had nothing to do with rescuing anyone.

Leon looked out the window in his office. Winter was coming, incrementally, and the clouds appeared to want to break open, to disguise the whole city with white snow. But it hadn't happened yet. Saving that woman's life seemed to bring him more clients. He was hitting everything on all six cylinders: work, fame, everything but Lil. The press asked Leon to go to the rescued woman's bedside at the hospital so they could do another story with more pictures. Leon declined. He wanted to allow the woman some privacy, to let her continue her life. Alice and George departed on their honeymoon to George's family home in Connecticut. Marco and Izzy teased Leon, saying, "Remember us? Your old friends from before you were famous." Even Mary Beach from the gallery stopped by with an armful of flowers, purple blooms with red at their centers. Alma had untangled them and placed them in a vase on her desk near her typewriter. They swayed as Leon passed them by. He had noticed that Mary Beach wore blue earrings veined with gold in the shapes of hearts as she bent to deliver the flowers to Alma. Ah, he thought, George's earrings. He was relieved it wasn't Lil. No one else knew about them. It was an accounting secret.

The telephone near Alma was still ringing. Hidden in the clouds, he discerned a torn moon, out too early. He had saved a life while Leopold and Loeb had taken one. An unwilling sacrifice and its opposite. Both incidents had happened for no reason at all. Leon picked up the telephone receiver.

A woman's hoarse voice said, "Finally. Your telephone has been busy for days."

"You could have come by."

"I was too busy. Did I tell you about the woman who died accidentally in bathtub gin and didn't get to taste it?"

"Yes," he said. "I suppose she couldn't swim either."

"Very funny," she said. She paused. "At my screen test I made lots of exaggerated expressions with my face and hands to show happiness, sadness, horror, and the hardest one of all, innocence." She couldn't help reenacting some of the facial expressions as she told him. "And guess what? They loved it and think I'm going to be in the movies."

"I hope you'll like being famous." Leon meant it and wondered. She didn't know the difficult parts. He was tired of marriage proposals from women his grandmother's age. "You'll have to show me what you did for the test." Then he whispered, "In private, of course."

~

Art Exhibit is All Sticks and Stones

New York City's Phillips Gallery's latest exhibit is called "American Abstracts." Among the pieces are unusual experimental works by Arthur Dove, who uses wax emulsion, twigs, pebbles, and newsprint on glass or metal. Dove says that his art is based on forms found in nature and he calls his abstractions "extractions" because he believes they focus on the essence of everything. Otto Dix has a sullen yet luminous and frightening painting of skulls filled with maggots. George Bellows is showing "Dempsey and Firpo," a moody piece about the two fighters in a boxing ring. The exhibit is varied and exciting and recommended for those seeking the unusual.

~

Lil had practiced the facial expressions she had seen at the movies in front of her mirror for days. She liked her mock horror one the most, with her mouth a large O, her hands splayed in the air, her dark bob fanning out, her brown eyes opened wide and then squeezed shut. Her eyebrows lifted into dark, curved half-circles. It had worked, all that imitation. They had liked it, told her to expect a contract, money, attention, soon. It was new. And it involved money. In this way she was a creation of her time.

Lil had gone out last week while Leon was busy, and picked up a sailor at the five-and-dime, in front of the soda boy who liked her. The sailor was aggressively muscular and his uniform was an insignificant scrap against his hulking body. He had a boyish face and sandy hair. He was browsing through girlie magazines while drinking a soda. Lil lay her hand across his as he was turning a page.

"My name's Lil. We could get a snort at my place."

The sailor didn't say much. But at her apartment she showed him her art and he said, "It don't mean much to me."

"It doesn't mean much to most people." Lil peeled off her clothes. "But I want you to tie me down and when you're done, cut my wrists."

The sailor laughed. "Times aren't that hard."

She had to show him how to tie her, scattering the yellow flowers of her sheets. But he tied her loosely, and when he was done all she was left with was a few bruises in places people couldn't see.

"I could of used a beer," the sailor said.

Lil threw his clothes at him. "Get out of here. Just get out now."

"You're an odd quiff," the sailor said, throwing some money on the floor, which Lil tied in a piece of old linen and placed into a drawer after he left.

The knock at her door was Mary Beach and Beatrice. Lil gave Beatrice cookies and let her play in another room with some toys Lil had bought at the five-and-dime. They could hear her singing while she was playing. Lil arranged Mary's pose, the fluttering white dress over her white scar, the fabrics of the background that leaked into one another like anecdotes that Lil wanted to tell. She reached for a cigarette but couldn't paint and smoke at the same time. This way, she thought, there would be no residue. Mary and I would both leave this room unchanged. Hopefully, it was the image that would endure. And how lucky Mary was to have Beatrice.

"Please take off those earrings," Lil told her, not knowing anything about them but their color. Mary irritated her, as well as being someone who made her feel closer to George in a way that Alice couldn't.

Mary slowly removed the blue lapis earrings, pooled them in her palm and rested them gently on a table covered with magazines. Mary was the only one who knew, from her husband, that they were part of George's debt to her husband's gang. A debt which was growing enormous by the minute.

"We're nearly finished with this portrait." She touched Mary's red hair as she straightened the tilted head. George entered Lil's mind and stayed. Lil wanted to stroke Mary's hair as though it was George's.

"So this'll be the last session?"

"Yes. Someday I hope Beatrice will let me paint her." Lil was already fervently painting, the white dress like snow and winter, with its absence and intrinsic cold. She thought of Leon, with his kind, solicitous face, how he would be fine, no matter what happened between them. He had done what was necessary and that was enough to be considered heroic. He was solid that way. She wanted to laugh. Heroic acts were continuing every day. Her mother had been heroic, for a while, getting them through the day-to-day no matter how sad she felt. Maybe she just got tired. Lil stopped and looked back at her work. "George will like this. It has a seasonal history." She smiled.

"He'll be surprised," Mary offered.

"I'm sure he assumes that it'll be Izzy or Marco or a model's portrait that he'll get." The red reminded Lil of lipstick kisses left on the illicit places of a body, territorial animal markings. She liked the coarseness of the strokes. Mary's body was shaky, yet touchable. She enjoyed the irony.

"George believes so many things, and lots of them ain't true."

Lil was interested. "Like what?" She wiped off her brushes, began cleaning up, sat down. She lit a cigarette.

"I'll tell you why I'm at the gallery, watching George, and even he don't know that's why I'm there. But you got to promise not to tell anyone."

"I promise." Lil's word was always good and Mary knew that.

Mary whispered everything to her. About her husband's

bootlegging business and loans, the night she got her scar (she was seventeen years old), and the way that these debts (the kind that George owed) were usually collected. Mary whispered that whatever she and George had was brief and over. She knew Lil would make sure that George stayed out of trouble and paid her husband. Alice didn't seem to have that kind of strength or focus, except in painting. "I'd hate to see George hurt. He's been swell."

Lil listened attentively. She wasn't shocked, but she felt sad. "I'll do what I can without telling anyone."

Then Beatrice, hearing so much talking, pushed open the door to the studio. A teddy bear was tucked under one of her arms, and a painted yo-yo dangled from the fingers of her other arm. Her thin ribs poked through her yellow dress and her red hair flew behind her as she dashed around the room, dancing.

"Can we go home now?" Beatrice asked her mother and then she ran to Lil who scooped her up in her arms.

Lil hugged her, kissing her all over her face smeared with milk and cookies. "Beatrice, you are wonderful and I'll never let you go." And they both did one of Beatrice's little dances together.

"Painting is about how things are revealed," Alice said, glancing at Lil and George at the Chinese restaurant. She pulled her brown wool sweater that smelled of camphor and turpentine onto her shoulders. Her honeymoon had been fine, there just hadn't been enough time for painting. George had been nervous and distracted, as if he didn't know what to do with himself since he didn't take many photographs anymore.

"I hope you don't mind that we must give up the apartment and live on the houseboat," he had said to her one evening over dinner.

"All the better to escape," Alice replied. But George didn't laugh. She didn't know anything about George's sexual shenanigans or money problems and she didn't want to. She didn't really mind the boat as long as there was room to paint and sketch. He knew that about her. She briefly wondered about the anatomy of the boat engine or the architecture of sails (canvas and air merging). Alice thought of migration and birds swarming toward warmth and light, their instincts guiding them, flooding their bodies until they shook with need. It sounded familiar.

"What are you working on?" Leon politely asked Alice at the Chinese restaurant. All sixteen diners at other tables had bought Leon their favorite dishes and sent them over because they recognized him from the newspapers. He knew Alice's painting had something to do with fruit. He ate part of a sweet and sour chicken that aptly described their mood at the table. His arm touched Lil's but she seemed far away, preoccupied.

"Melons: watermelons, cantaloupes, crenshaw, casaba, honeydew melons. Their wonderful, large, round shapes, the seeds and the whole complicated city living inside of them. I'm doing one painting of seeds and juice only." Her hands danced in the air, fell to the white sheet of the table, and met the chow mein.

"How was your honeymoon?" Marco's gold tooth

winked.

"This is a time of coming and going or going and coming back." Lil smiled sarcastically, then she shuffled through the food as if she were searching for the perfect supper. The large, black buttons on her dress contained every color, absorbing them all.

For a moment Lil wondered about Chinese culture, the chopsticks, the jade, red lanterns, food, their written language. Were they older than the Egyptians? Did they share some symbols? In America there were new manufactured goods, mass-produced dinnerware, lipsticks, pens, paper, and how the Palmer method of penmanship had been lost. Those glorious things that verged on art itself.

Lil looked at George. She wanted his arms around her. She'd do anything to have that. Lil thought of Alice, in her own world, one of melons, painting, comfortable furniture, and lastly George and his antics. Alice had insulated herself already.

"Actually," George said, "a funny thing happened on our honeymoon at the lake in Connecticut." His mustache twisted. Alice looked at him. "Alice and I were wading in our swimsuits and the same policeman that had fined Audrey and me jumped out again from behind some bushes. He was disappointed that we were wearing clothes. I said, 'Haven't I seen you somewhere before?' 'No,' he said loudly and then he left, looking quite chastised, didn't he, Alice?"

Alice nodded. Izzy was half sleeping behind her, underneath a red dragon lantern. Her sequined dress shifted with her limbs, sending out light in dots and dashes, her own, tired Morse code.

"You could have pushed him into the lake," Marco added. "My favorite kind of bulls are the wet and angry ones." Izzy kneaded his arm.

"And then who would have rescued him if he couldn't swim? Would Leon have made the trip? Because I can't swim," George asked.

"I can't swim either," Lil said.

"Neither can I," Izzy added.

"That just leaves Alice, me, and the famous Leon Shaffer, swimmer extraordinaire," Marco said. "I can't believe you never learned, George."

"I never did, although several of my sisters did."

Alice's brown sleeve dipped into a gift of egg foo young and turned a darker brown. She tried to wipe off the gravy with her napkin. George took his napkin and helped her. "There," he said. "Better?"

"I'm not a child," Alice said matter-of-factly. All five pairs of eyes at the table turned to her. "Sometimes you're as understanding as a rubber ball."

"I know you're more interested in your paintings than the messy details of life," George countered. He wasn't perturbed, eating some Chinese noodles with sauce clinging to his mustache.

"Which is better for the gallery business anyway," Lil couldn't help saying.

"True," George said. "Except that this will be my last exhibition for a while. I'm going to secretly close the gallery. It'll be temporary. But none of you can say anything about this to anyone."

They all looked at one another and then at George. Lil

sucked in her breath, wanted a cigarette, was surprised, but shouldn't have been. The air was gone from the room. She knew that she and Alice might vanish without the gallery to show their paintings. At least temporarily, since it was difficult for women painters to find places to show their work. The moving pictures became more important, for the money, and to be certain that she hadn't disappeared or been forgotten like a dress you once loved but was left hanging in the back of the closet. She realized that she could fade away, like Alice. That she was afraid she'd become Alice, and then she shook her head. She still had a choice.

Leon started to ask Lil if she was cold and would she like her sweater, and then he stopped, thinking better of it because of George and Alice. He wanted to change the subject, so he whispered, "There's gossip about suicide." So only Lil could hear.

Lil was startled. She wondered what other people suspected. Her hand shook as she reached for her cup of tea. "About George?"

Leon laughed. "No, silly, about Leopold and Loeb." He was louder. "I read it in the newspaper."

"How did we get to talking about them?"

Leon had been about to say something else. "I don't know." He felt defeated. No matter what he said, he revealed his interest. "I guess I was thinking about things that don't last. It's something I'm not familiar with in my work. The numbers don't go anywhere. They last forever and they're final." Unless you manipulated them, which Leon wouldn't do.

"Temporarily closed," George repeated.

Lil decided that when she was in the motion pictures she'd play a young girl who wore a tricorne hat that was too big and kept falling into her eyes. She'd wear lipstick, and a long, baggy dress that would cover her knobby knees. She'd ride her bicycle, gingerly ringing the bell. Apples and bread would fill up her basket. She would go to a river park and abandon her bicycle behind a tree in order to watch a couple necking passionately. She would practice kissing the tree, watching how the man and woman intertwined. She was still too young to understand these things. She would never understand how she ended up filled with a baby.

Everyone stared uncomfortably at the napkins covering their laps. Lil was surrounded by cigarette smoke. Alice unraveled a string of yarn from her sweater and tied it around her finger. Izzy rubbed her throat as if to be certain that it was still there. Marco rolled a stray peanut from one of the dishes between his fingers. Leon was leaning toward Lil, his hand on her arm as though he wanted to say something but hadn't gotten around to it yet. He was obscured by his own, private, cigarette smoke cloud. George was the only one eating. He took small bites from all the dishes. He wanted to taste a little of everything.

"Everyone thinks their bad luck is temporary," someone said.

~

Peter Pan Flies

The ever-popular Jerome Kern has written two songs for the adapted Broadway musical "Peter Pan" that opened

last night. Written by J.M. Barrie, the play was full of swashbuckling fun as the magical boy, Peter Pan, refused to grow up and traveled to Neverland with all the Darling children. Tinker Bell was acted by V.B. Faire and all the playgoers seemed to enjoy this theatrical production, giving it a standing ovation.

~

Leon placed his fortune cookie in the hollow of Lil's belly button as she lay naked on her bed. She couldn't help giggling as he broke open the cookie without using his hands. His tongue snaked the cookie into his mouth and he chewed. The pieces fell onto her bare stomach, the tiny strip of paper tickled.

"Aha," he said, reading it as he hovered over her, wearing his duck canvas trousers, garters, socks, and suspenders. "I'll find true love."

"Where will you find it, Leon? Does the fortune tell you that?" She laughed. "Maybe here?" and she pointed to the triangle of dark hair between her legs. "Or here?" and she pointed to her small, jaunty breasts. "Certainly not here," and she pushed back the hair from her head so it reached the top of her pillow as a dark shadow.

Leon ate the cookie pieces, leaving the fortune on her stomach. Their clothes were left in soft piles around the bed. Their bodies tangled again. His arm gripped her spine like a life vest that stopped him from sinking. Her small hipbones slid beneath his. His body carried too much flesh. She seemed tiny and shy underneath him. His hands crawled through her dark hair as he pushed into her and she cried out.

Afterwards, as he lay by her, he wondered if she thought of George, and finally he didn't care. He had done all he could do. He was a hero, after all, at least to other people. Was Lil the one he had been looking for?

But then he couldn't help himself. He touched her sheets, blooming with tiny yellow flowers that now seemed scattered. He lost her outline, her definition in the hazy cigarette smoke that circled her. "It's difficult for me to imagine George and Alice floating on an ocean somewhere." Like flotsam.

"Yes," her face turned toward him but he could only see parts of it. "And I suppose that you, of all people, would know about his financial problems."

"Yes, but I can't talk about that. It's confidential."

"I assume you know already that it's Mary Beach's husband he owes all that money to. He borrowed money from a bootlegger. And for what? Gallery debts, some gambling, fancy gifts?" She sighed and inhaled at the same time. "He has no imagination." She had never received any gifts from George, not even someone else's art that she liked. She crushed her cigarette in a silver ashtray that had a dog on point at its edge. "He'll hate it on the boat." She slid under the covers. "He knows nothing about repairs and I could just see him trying to balance on a boat while he's printing some negatives or something." But Lil imagined him catching her as the deck tipped, complicated shadows in violet and deep blue dappling their clothes, sun discovering the spaces between their clothes and skin. He would tell her all the names of the nearby rivers and lakes as they floated on the sea. Alice was left on shore somewhere, shopping or painting. Or gone. They didn't have to talk, George and Lil. They didn't need to say anything to one another. "At least he's thinking about taking up photography again."

She was tiring of her time with Leon. The second life she was supposed to want but didn't. She thought of the moon, shriveled and white in this cold city outside her clear window. How beautiful it would appear, hovering over someplace warmer, poised over George's boat, a blank, round canvas waiting for her brush. She could read to him about the Impressionists until his seasickness passed. She would describe the natives and their customs in whatever exotic land they had chosen to live in, at least for a while. She would confess that she knew about Mary Beach as well as Mary's husband. She and George could go anywhere, have a gallery in an obscure European village, arrange for models that neither of them could understand. They could arrange the models using gestures. They could take photographs and make paintings in another language. At night they would swim into one another, feel for anchors.

"Do you love him?" He tried asking the back of her dark hair, staining a pillow. He wondered if she was faking being asleep since she hardly ever slept.

"Do love or art really matter, except to the people doing them?" Her back and shoulders protected her. She pushed further underneath the covers, drifting in the warming sheets. She'd wait for the turbulence and waves to subside before stepping out, before walking on land again.

The celebrity telephone calls about the near drowning incident were subsiding and Leon threw himself furiously into
his work. Restless papers filled with columns of numbers
buried him. In his dreams he was trapped under large nines,
zeroes, and ones and couldn't dig his way out. He had more
clients and a copious amount of work. Alma flirted shame-
lessly with clients when she had the time. Her lips formed
little smiles that said yes. She asked Leon, "What's that
smell from your jacket? Turpentine?" The winter cold and
the beginnings of snow suited her, made her puffed, red lips
more noticeable. Everyone began to smell of damp wool.

Leon finally got Mr. Beach on the telephone. He was quiet as Leon laid out George's case for paying him back. Finally a gruff, slow voice said, "It's due when I say it's due. And
it ain't negotiable." Mr. Beach wanted to say that neither
was his wife. He pulled out his hand-painted necktie that
had women in taffeta skirts dancing along the length of it,
and then he stuffed it back underneath his jacket. He hung
up the telephone. He'd read about this man, Leon Shaffer,
a hero in the newspapers, and his wife had taken a shine to
the guy and brought him expensive flowers. Even Beatrice,
little Beatrice, had crayoned Leon's face once on his morning newspaper.

Leon watched the city traffic dodging the first flutter of
snow. The running boards, tonneaus, handles, and even the
distraught headlights were submerged under the snow and
then appeared again as the cars drove off. Snow flew off into
distilled piles. Leon missed the summer and the warmth already, when street games expanded from block to block and

children ran untethered on the hot New York pavement. A few flakes caught on his window. They melted quickly into wet streaks on the glass. His heater clanked and then hissed, letting Leon know that it, too, was working hard.

What he had wished for in Lil he had accidentally received himself. He saw now that people went wherever their hearts led them, no matter how ridiculous or insane. He didn't want to believe in something as abstract as fate. It wasn't scientific or mathematical. It couldn't be proven or shown to be true on graph paper. He was starting to realize that there wasn't much difference between admiration and sacrifice. That the two were often intertwined.

Alma knocked on his office door and rushed in with an envelope and handed it to Leon. Her lips were a blur. Leon opened the note from the woman he had saved. She had just left the hospital, and it said: "What were you thinking when you saved me anyway? That everything would turn out just ducky?" He could picture her asking that and then running away to hide.

He thought he might try to visit her someday, when there were no longer any fans or photographers. He honestly hadn't been thinking at all.

Dr. Duncan asked Lil, "How is he?" Even Dr. Duncan knew that no one could ever truly know what went on inside someone else's mind. He could guess but he knew his own thoughts came expeditiously and left unceremoniously. Yet that was his job, to understand someone's mind, get to the core of their beliefs, to affect them. In Lil's world, he was the teacher that watched the paint positioned on the canvas, made suggestions and corrections, and when it was ready, he would exhibit it.

Lil's sherry-colored skirt draped the gray couch. She heard a faint knocking at the window, but when she looked it was a light snow that brushed the glass, not making a sound. It must have been the heels of her shoes. "I tried to dream last night..." She counted the stripes on Dr. Duncan's tie. She stopped at twenty-one for the blue stripes and she hadn't started yet on the flame-colored-ones. "...without sleeping." How many times had she tried counting sheep or birds or lions? His white linen suit settled in a chair as snow hurled itself at the window in sympathy.

"Is that better than sleeping without dreams?" His pencil tapped on his desk, replacing the noise of her heels.

"I wouldn't know." She knew she had a whole other life while most people slept, the painting, reading, thinking. Anything that was quiet. She tried to tiptoe barefoot around her apartment so she wouldn't disturb the neighbors. There were occasional creaks from another floor or shining lights in distant apartments that kept her company. She didn't mind anymore. She rarely slept. She had so much extra time, a whole lifetime in the night. "There were parrots, butterflies, monkeys, even bougainvillea." She smiled. "I was in a jungle. There was the scent of rain and tequila. Vines twisted and grew around me and held me. I was tied to a tree. I couldn't move. Then we spooned, he and I. It was exquisite!"

"Sometimes, if we don't sleep, it's difficult to tell what's real and what's not." Dr. Duncan's agitated pencil rose and then finally rested on his desk.

"Then I was lying in a field but the ground was the color of flamingoes. It was raining and I lay on my back and I left my mouth open and I kept on swallowing water. My belly swelled, but I didn't feel full. I'd heard once that turkeys drowned that way. He came and took my arm and told me to paint the sky, a nice, blue, sunny one. When I was done, it stopped raining and the sky was lovely, bright and sunny, just like in the painting. But when he kissed me and told me my painting was beautiful, all the water gushed out of my mouth, pouring over us both. A small fish flew out of my mouth and thrashed on the ground between us." She lit a cigarette and watched the smoke coil. "I do know the difference between what's real and what's not, Dr. Duncan." She inhaled and exhaled. "But lately I think about him often."

"Why do you think that is?"

"Sometimes I feel like a vessel to men. Just a way of working out something they want that's not necessarily me."

"And what is it that you want?"

"I want that furious tiny fish." She extinguished her cigarette and curled up on the couch. "Now that he's married I want him more," she admitted, her head underneath her hand, her voice peeping through.

"I thought we were talking about Leon." He leaned forward in his chair but Lil didn't notice.

"No, not Leon. George, it was always George. I think, Doctor, if I'm not fighting, I feel like I'm drowning." Her small, hoarse voice came out from below her dark hair. A foot dangled. She sighed, "Anyway, you can have the half-dreams if you want them."

"You promised not to stab yourself again and you've kept that promise to me and I appreciate it."

"It doesn't count if I get someone else to do it for me." Lil's skirt overflowed from the sofa as though some sherry had spilled there. One heel thrashed out from a shoe. "I miss the child terribly."

"What about the moving pictures?" He noted everything, the turn of her head, her every word. This was a sort of fame and attention, wasn't it? He would have to ask a colleague, decide what the dreams meant.

"I'm about to start a new painting. The movie studio knows where to find me if they want me." She sat up, the rustling skirt tucked under her legs. "I think our time is up." She would have to ask Mrs. Becker about this psychoanalysis again. Was it really worth it? As she made her way out the door, she said to him, "I don't need any excuses." And he wrote that down too.

~

"Lady Be Good" is Very Good

A new musical called "Lady Be Good" debuted last night at The Liberty Theatre in New York City. The play was written by Guy Bolton and Fred Thompson and the incredibly talented George and Ira Gershwin wrote the music. It is the story of a sister and brother who, both having gone broke, were willing to forfeit themselves to help each other. Fred Astaire and his sister Adele Astaire were in the starring roles, which made for an entertaining time.

The music, dancing, and story all worked well together and created a wonderful evening at the theatre.

~

As Lil exited a cab she could hear jazz locked inside an apartment near the sidewalk. She carried her life-sized, covered painting toward the gallery but she wanted to rest for a minute on the cold, dirty street. She placed her hands against the basement window, felt the rhythm. She remembered summer as different tunes she could hear people singing from apartment windows she walked by, while open fire hydrants flooded the streets. Sometimes she caught the first line of a popular song and then heard the following line from the next building. She distinguished the tune from all the other sounds, the children playing, women gossiping along the steps, balls bounced along the streets. In the winter, New York closed in on itself, tightened like a fist, and coal dust dirtied everything, snow, shoes, windows, car wheels. You'd have to dig people out, excavate their lives. Cold separated them, kept them inside, insulated. Clouds formed gray shadows, a tiny flicker of light here and there. People thoughtlessly bumped into her, their coats softening the impact. She moved her painting away from them. An empty tree reached into the sky from a square of chewed-up ground outside the gallery.

Lil dragged her canvas up the stairs. Maybe she'd learn to live in a foreign town where she'd know all her neighbors' first names, greet them, know too much about their likes and dislikes, learn to speak another language. She wouldn't

avoid the old woman who talked to herself, she'd eaves-
drop, discover the secrets that no one else cared to hear.
She'd make them her own, then learn from the old woman
how to sleep at night.

In the gallery there was an exhibit about man-made di-
sasters, paintings that pulsed with torn skin, veins, blood
and flesh slapped onto paper. A sculpture that represent-
ed war, all metal and sharp corners. Jars were filled with
pennies for the victims. A mixed media of the geology of
mankind's mistakes in layers, a Bosch painting categorizing
suffering into strata. It reminded Lil of why she didn't sleep,
all the things that had gone wrong and all the things that
could still go wrong. There was one more show after this
one, the women's show.

Lil glimpsed Mary Beach's red hair and her silhouette as
she hurried from a back room, her legs moving rapidly. Her
dark, sagging stockings made her look even younger in her
shapeless, two-toned suit, and boots. She was wiping her
mouth. When she turned toward Lil, Lil saw a rim of bruises
around her left eye. They weren't too dark or noticeable yet,
like grape juice that had stained a shirt, sunken below and
spread out. Mary came closer and Lil saw that she had applied a generous amount of powder and make-up to mute
the bruises. There wasn't much swelling. It had probably
happened a few days ago. Lil liked her and adored Beatrice.

"Does this exhibit give you nightmares?" Lil was grateful for staying awake all night because sleeping would have
given her nightmares.

Mary laughed. "Hardly." Sometimes it was harder at
home, Mary thought.

"I'm here to surprise George." Lil put down the painting and removed her coat.

"He'll be surprised, I'm sure." Mary twisted a boot on the floor. "I ain't going to be here much longer. Today's my last day at the gallery."

Lil held Mary's chin up toward the ceiling. "He's merciless. Just like this exhibit." Lil knew that it wasn't a good sign for George's situation that Mary was leaving.

"My big cheese husband took a painting on credit. Just to annoy George or to be sure George would pay him back and not beef about it." She pointed to a far wall, a large gouache of an alley with empty bottles, overfilled garbage cans, and a figure beaten down between the newspapers and trash.

"Social commentary." Lil's hand brushed the rhinestone buttons on her dress. "I hope it was worth it and that you've paid your husband back for those bruises." She looked at Mary's red hair.

"It reminds George that my husband bumps people off without thinking about it. Now George probably knows about me." Mary pulled on one of her stockings. "He probably feels like he's left holding the bag." She sighed.

"But the gallery did have its benefits." Both women laughed, but Mary's eye hurt and she stopped laughing.

"Tell Beatrice she can visit me anytime. Tell her she's the cat's whiskers. And I'd still like to do a portrait of her someday." Lil kissed Mary on her cheek.

"Thanks. It's good to meet someone on the level. Beatrice likes you too. I don't know much about art, but you seem like the real McCoy."

Lil dug in her pocket and removed the old linen neatly

tied around the sailor's money and handed it to Mary. Otherwise she might have given it to George. "For Beatrice's future. It's not much but it's something."

"I ain't going to take this." Mary pushed it away. "I can't."

Lil forced the tight package into Mary's hands. "Think of it as your modeling fee. It's for both of you. Hide it. Take it, please."

Mary kissed Lil's cheek. "I'll watch for you in the moving pictures." Mary curled her fur stole, a fox's head complete with dried, shriveled eyes and a mouth hanging down from her throat, around her shoulders. Her wedding ring sparkled as her fingers nestled in the soft fur.

"It'll probably be something like 'Pretty Sinners' or 'Daddy's Little Girl' or maybe, if I'm lucky, it'll be 'The Artist's Good Time,'" Lil complained.

"How about 'My Whoopee Night in Paris?'" Mary waved as she stepped out the door. "Good luck. Thanks." And she was gone.

George's mustache appeared, twitched a little, and then he scurried to a back room. "Mary," he bellowed although she had already left.

Lil walked past the accidents, murders, robberies, and war on the walls and found George in the storage room wedged between stacks of paintings. "She's thrown you over. She's gone for good." She ran an arm along the back of his distracted neck. "I'm here now."

He bent down, moved a tiny watercolor of a blooming landscape. The flowers were mere dots of color. "What are you doing here?" George remembered that the artist who did the landscape had been lovely too. When he stood he looked down into Lil's eyes, and he saw himself in her dark irises. He had forgotten how small she was. She was a book with a page that he returned to again and again, forgetting how good and yet how complicated she was, and he was surprised each time. He didn't need to see the totality, for, as in life, that could mean something completely different from the various parts. He could easily live in the segments.

"I have something for you. Something you asked for." Lil wondered for a moment what Norma Talmadge, the elegant and glamorous actress, would do. Lil lifted her dress, the glass buttons knocking softly against one another. She watched George's face, a series of vignettes. Alice was sweet and innocuous and Lil felt suddenly bad. Lil thought that perhaps she was going insane, waiting for George. George's face settled into a weak leer.

"I'm busy," he said, but Lil had reached up to kiss him, pulled down her bloomers and wrapped her legs around him. He could feel the heels of her feet meeting at his back. He feebly pushed her away, but she clung to him. He could feel his belt buckle embossing her thigh so he removed it. He fumbled for a condom in a nearby drawer half filled with etchings. After he had fucked her, not too hurriedly, and he had muffled her cry with his palm, he checked his paintings. None had been harmed. Some had been knocked a little out of place, but he moved them back. He said, "Don't be delusional about this."

She straightened her dress. "Why don't the people I let inside of me want to stay?"

"People are casual and complacent these days, including

you, my dear little Lil, including you."

"Maybe they're afraid that I'm too dangerous." She was talking to herself.

"I'm thinking about Alice." He once had a nightmare where he felt a sense of guilt about an act he was accused of committing but hadn't actually done. He had done something similar, but lesser, and he had already forgotten what it was. He never recalled what the horrible act was in his dream. He looked away from her, out toward the front door as though he hoped someone would enter and save him. "I hear a customer."

Lil's heels clicked into the gallery where she stood by her painting. George's eyes wavered between her face and the covered artwork. No one was there, no one had entered or caught them. Lil wasn't that much taller than her painting. She removed the cloth.

George gasped at the wild portrait of Mary Beach. "They say all portraits are self-portraits," he murmured. "Hmm, Mary Beach." The unhindered brushstrokes, the stamina of the colors. Mary was an odalisque in white with her red hair aflame, entertaining the viewer. The expression on her face was one of weariness, as though she was tired of the indisputable progress of time, at how long it took the painter to complete the picture, wondering when it would all be over. It was an expression George had never seen on Mary in real life. The trace of a scar began at her ankle and slithered up her leg to below her dress. Colors insisted on becoming abstract objects around her, a pillow, drapes. The suggestion of an orange placed near her outstretched hand reminded George of Alice, hinting that Mary could grasp Alice, eat her at will. But it was the face that drew the viewer in again and again, a portrait of too much memory, even with an unclarified mouth, resigned eyes, a nose like something that had lingered underwater too long. "This is a wonderful portrait for my last exhibit here."

"I told you I'd do a portrait." She had originally wanted to toss Mary into his face, into Alice's face also, but it had not worked out that way.

"It's so wonderfully... demented and inventive, most continental." George stood back and enjoyed it. It was a flirtation, an invitation to tell this woman something that she didn't already know, show her something that hadn't been done before. The portrait led to the painter. "We won't say a word about any of this, to anyone," he emphasized.

Lil was tired, suddenly very tired. He could have been a figment of her imagination. She walked to the door of the gallery. "A word about what?" She left, not getting everything she had wanted. She could hear a police siren or an ambulance racing down the street. She would rest before she started another painting. It was snowing outside. Her path would soon be erased behind her.

"It's the nature of wood to float," Alice calmly rested her hand against the white stern of the thirty-five-foot houseboat moored at the Sag Harbor Yacht Club. She watched the sleek lines of a powerboat racing through the harbor, a cluster of nervous sailboats, their sails tipped to the side, like women with white scarves gossiping. Alice wore two sweaters, a faded orange one that could be seen through the mesh of a flowered one, whose stems and leaves had become mere threads. It was cold but clear and sunny.

"She was built in 1904. Her name, 'Shi,' is the Chinese word for both persimmons and business," George explained.

Alice laughed good-naturedly, but she could feel small waves against the sides at night. The motion reminded her of rocking a nonexistent baby.

Lil glanced at Alice's disintegrating sweaters and whispered to Leon, "I'd be surprised if this works out."

As if George had overheard her, he said, "There's a view, a map, time to recover from anything and everything, and Alice has her painting. What more could we ask for?"

"I see that you have that rounded 'sprung' roof that's so popular right now," Leon said to George. They moved inside from the short deck, stepping through the galley door. They walked down six old oak steps into a square, almost empty, room with boxes, a chair, strewn painting supplies, and a few blank canvases. The window showed the water, the horizon, distant land, levels of pale colors. The canvas below it showed a reflective window filled with snow. It was too quiet, Leon thought. The day's weather would determine what their plans would be. Today was tame, cold.

"Yes, they replaced the roof recently but we still cook and have light by kerosene, and pump all our water by hand. It's an adventure, right, Alice dear?" But George wasn't really interested in the details of the ship.

Alice was sorting through several boxes and retrieved some cups. She hoped she wouldn't see any rats scurrying along the dock near the pump. "Would you two like some-

THE BOHEMIANS169

thing to drink?" she asked Leon and Lil who sat on some boxes. Their backs were curved like card players hunched over their secretive hands. Light swam onto the walls in navigational indifference and then left. The light was the color of lost moths.

"Water, please," Lil said in her rough voice.

"Thanks, but I brought my own." Leon took a flask out of his jacket pocket and poured a little into one of the proffered cups. He looked around and wondered if this was called "Running for Your Life." He peered into a bathroom, or "head," as they were called on boats, the size of his desk at work. Alice left to get water and in the silence Leon could hear the water outside asking questions of the boat. Not receiving any answers, it asked again and again. "How long do you plan to stay in this marina, George?"

Lil looked at George. She was waiting for his answer.

Alice returned, the wooden door creaking. She handed Lil her water. "I want to go somewhere I can see fruit growing. I want to see the source of the fruit."

"This is quite different from living in New York." George sipped from Leon's flask. He wiped his mustache. "I've heard that Izzy is becoming a sensation there."

"Yes, up in Harlem," Leon said.

Lil saw two Alices sitting on boxes, one superimposed over the other, Cubist, both wearing the same frayed clothes. She blinked. She was tired and Dr. Duncan had warned her about long-term insomnia, the false and flickering images, dreams you could have while awake. "That's fine," she had told the doctor. "I'll have more choices, more ways to see." Who was she trying to convince? Her studio was languishing right now. She hoped to use gouache next because it dried fast. She'd have to work quickly, think quickly. She missed her heart-shaped palette, the oozing paint. "Seeing is still a verb. I'm not worried," she had last told the doctor.

"We think the man living in the large houseboat over there," George pointed to a berth at the end of the dock near the rugged house on shore, "is probably a bootlegger. We see lots of people coming and going there."

Lil thought about the reflections from water, how the images were similar to what they reflected, but ultimately different. Some of the details differed in the act of reflecting so that the viewer forgot the moon had certain craters or that the stars were jagged and brittle. There was the evidence and how it was perceived, two completely different viewpoints. Lil watched as one of the Alices went over to George and ran her fingers through his hair. Her trajectory from the box on which she was sitting remained in the air as a wave of light. Lil felt this Alice taunting her; Alice's sparkling wedding ring was an accusation in George's gray hair. The other Alice stayed on the box, crossed her ankles, her mud-colored trousers becoming too short. One Alice scratched her arm. Lil blinked again and the second Alice was still quietly sitting on an unopened box. The water outside rose into small, corrugated waves like blue linen napkins prepared for a special dinner.

"These are strange times we live in," Lil said. "How do two artists like sharing space with a bootlegger?" She looked out past the dock, toward a pergola with the "Sag Harbor Yacht" sign on top.

"Well, we are similar in some ways. We both enjoy entertaining guests," George answered.

"Except that drinking wears off too quickly and people need to come back for more," Leon said. He still wasn't sure whether he liked George or not, even when George was struggling. Some days he did, other days he didn't want to help him at all. But George knew how to make a woman feel special. Leon could see that. George just needed to decide which woman.

"For art, you must surrender yourself completely, and it lasts forever." Alice looked at Lil. Art makes you content, she thought, and at least you learn from it.

"Which one is that?" Lil looked at George, wanting him to flood her, kiss her, let the caresses leak in. But she knew that wouldn't happen now. "One makes certain you don't have to think any more than you need to. I like that." She allowed her weariness to wash over her until she didn't feel tired anymore. Reality was jumbled and slipping away like someone accidentally locked in a house that was boarded up against winter. Or a man who fell asleep in a chair while eating an apple that tumbled from his hand, bounced slightly on the floor, and wasn't seen again. "We invent our own meanings anyway." Was she talking about her sanity or her painting? Were they different?

That night, while Leon slept and Lil wandered around her apartment alone and on tiptoe, she thought she smelled saltwater everywhere.

Broken Color

"Marriages send me over the edge." Mrs. Becker was seated among a group of tables and chairs. The choreography of waiters around Mrs. Becker and Lil amused them at their luncheon. A crystal chandelier, suspended from the painted ceiling at the Plaza Hotel restaurant, tossed refracted light and subdued colors against the pale walls. The room resembled a French chateau. Mrs. Becker peered at one of the leaf-shaped crystals overhead and saw herself reflected in it. "Including my own marriage."

Mrs. Becker had been privy to some of George's romps because some of them took place on the grounds of the Beckers' country house. She thought of that new woman, Mary something, with her lovely red hair. She heard she had a pretty child, a daughter. That Mary was from new money. One of those people who was shocked by their sudden good fortune, determined to spend it. The money was usually gone in a year or two.

"I can't imagine Alice and George disappearing to some foreign country," Lil said, wondering what it would have been like to have Mrs. Becker as her mother, instead of the woman who cried constantly, sunken into the family sofa, and then applied make-up so her fly boy wouldn't notice her swollen eyes. A mother who, near the end, decided that the light hurt her skin and made her want to vanish. And

she did. Now Lil used that same light for her paintings. Mrs. Becker's two grown children were living in Europe and hadn't been home in years. Mrs. Becker helped young artists instead.

"Mr. Becker and I wanted to help George with the gallery. To keep it from closing. But his debts were too extreme, with all that borrowing. Apparently there was also some gambling. Mr. Becker had looked into it." She drew her napkin onto her lap, hoisted her water glass to her lips and drank. She put down her goblet and pressed the ornate silverware with her fingertips. "How is Dr. Duncan?"

Lil thought of all those impossible, lost afternoon hours. To the doctor, people were revealed through their thoughts, words, and gestures. How do you fix the ruined? Or the ones hypnotized by past events and who are destined to reenact them over and over? Those memories were caught in Lil's body. The doctor's gray couch had begun to sag under her weight and she didn't think Mrs. Becker even knew about her suicide attempt, when she had stabbed herself with one of her sharper palette knives. It was momentary and too difficult. She had those tiny scars. "Fine. He listens. Sometimes I think he's a good audience, and sometimes I think he's a bad one."

"I don't know what that means precisely, but I do know that he will improve your art and your life. He certainly helped me." She superciliously stabbed a piece of lettuce with her fork. Her black gloves lay politely collapsed on the tablecloth. Pearls circled her neck. "Have you heard how Leopold and Loeb stuffed a gag in that poor Franks boy's mouth and then hit him on the skull with a chisel for

no reason?" Her eyes grew wide and then rested on Lil's
long, layered, orange dress. Mrs. Becker had hoped for one
of her more alarming outfits, to razz the diners at this old,
established hotel, to remind them another era had begun.
Mrs. Becker and Lil received more attention from the waiters when Lil, the kind of woman that men noticed, dressed
extravagantly. The additional consideration was either from
curiosity, attraction, or the wish to have them gone soon.

"Leon and I went to a King Tutankhamen exhibit and
now we think of events in terms of willing or unwilling
sacrifices. King Tut was a willing sacrifice but his slaves
weren't. Bobby Franks was definitely an unwilling sacrifice. And that woman that Leon rescued might have been a
willing one." Lil thought of her mother swaying, suspended
from the ceiling. No one knew about the child. Lil had never
told anyone, except Dr. Duncan. And she tried not to think
about him anymore.

"Sacrificed for what?" Mrs. Becker had to signal the
waiter to get more water.

"Oh, it varies. Art, love, politics, money, often religion.
Take your choice. In the old days the sacrifices were virgins
or animals killed to appease the gods. Now, sometimes, we
must appease different gods. And they're angry about art,
love, politics, money, or religion."

"Well, anyway," Mrs. Becker buttered her bread, watching as Lil collapsed a piece into her mouth. Sometimes it
was disgusting watching people eat, she thought. The
light's clarity was too proficient. "Clarence Darrow has been
pontificating in the courtroom for weeks now and the trial
seems to be all about the brain. As well as Freud and mental

illness. Clarence Darrow called Leopold a paranoiac with a manic drive and Loeb a terrible schizophrenic. He said that a governess forced sex on Leopold when he was fourteen and a chauffeur did the same for Loeb. They're both very intelligent but emotionally halted at the age of seven. It's a very interesting trial. I'll have to ask Dr. Duncan what he makes of it."

It was a late November afternoon. There was the sound of ringing and shuffling as the waiters hurried, as china touched glass. Silverware glared. For comfort, Lil wanted to touch Mrs. Becker's hand underneath the white tablecloth, but the nest of Mrs. Becker's hair and her stiff dress stopped her. Mrs. Becker was a woman her mother's age that Lil already knew she wouldn't grow to resemble. She latticed her fingers. Lil didn't much care what Dr. Duncan thought, because it wouldn't change anything, certainly not the past, and she was dubious about the future. "Now he's a willing sacrifice."

"Who?" Mrs. Becker asked. "Dr. Duncan?"

"No," Lil said. "George."

~

Female Help Wanted

Stenographer with dictaphone experience for sales department of an old established firm. Desire reliable, educated woman with good appearance, 28-40. Will make attractive offer to right party. 20 Central Bldg.

~

Leon noticed that Lil had lost her brazenness, her certainty in everything around her, just as his fame was waning. She tested a chair before she sat in it. She touched her food before she ate it. She had taken to clutching the arm of the person she spoke to as though she wanted to be sure they were really there, that they actually existed. Her mind defied gravity, outwitted ideas, racing from one subject to another. She claimed her shoes were following her. She said her table regarded her critically and then moved itself. She complained at night to her own flower-encrusted sheets and she wandered through her apartment, alighting in her studio, but by morning she hadn't painted anything new. She was more Bohemian by being less than herself.

Leon fell asleep to the rattle of her slippers, her boa twined around her arms as she left the room. When he woke up, a coarse voice from the beautiful, small woman with the dark, skittery bob said, "I've been in a moving picture show all night."

"Did the studio call?"

"No, not yet." But she had seen private movies on her apartment walls. Her eyes felt as though they were melting. The images were as insubstantial as rain and she knew it. It was as though she had materialized in another world, the Egyptian's other world, a netherworld entirely. The fragments were silent moving pictures, greeting her as she turned a corner into her kitchen (along the cabinets), or her studio (against the blank walls and canvases), as she glanced upward from her bed (above the headboard), or even in her bathroom (reflected in her faucets or mirror). She fitted some under her tongue, others were the size of doors, or the height of another human being. They were shadow and light, intermezzo without the music, grainy without substance. There was no smell except for the lingering bitter odor of tea that Lil had drunk that morning. She couldn't taste these figures, touch a shoulder, pry their mouths open, share Chinese food.

She didn't think she was in these movies exactly, but once a small, dark girl climbed a tree, fell, stood up and smoothed her dress. Once a couple kissed and the woman rubbed her arms along the man's sides and Lil thought they were her own hands until she noticed that the woman had blonde hair. She wondered if she was in someone else's dream. For these apparitions mostly happened at night, during the time everyone else was asleep.

Once a man in a suit and cloak turned to Lil, a dove appearing on his arm, as he pulled scarves from his sleeves. She thought he would flip a coin out of her ear, but it seemed he was gesturing to someone else, a shadowy audience, a mother and child. Once Leon caught her trying to talk to one of them in her studio when he went to the bathroom, but they usually didn't speak to Lil. They were ghosts, thin biographies. Mostly Lil felt invisible.

"I smell smoke," she had told the magician.

"But there's no fire," the magician had smiled. "Unless you make one," he mouthed back to her just before Leon asked her what she was doing and who she was talking to.

"I have too many people inside of me," Lil said once.

"Everyone does," Leon answered gently.

Lil's canvas sat there, unpainted. These people seemed to be waiting for a conversation to begin. She kissed Leon at his jawbone, his leonine hair falling onto his face, his hazel eyes closed, his nose perfectly triangular. She told him to go back to sleep. She wanted to explain this strange phenomenon to herself before she shared it with anyone else.

Lil, for her part, pretended to be sure again. During the day she tried to surreptitiously feel a chair with her hand before she sat in it. She turned the knob on a door before she passed through it. That was after she had walked into a wall believing there was a door there, one made of darkness and light. No one had seen her. She felt for roundness and sharpness, flatness and texture, shape and temperature. Then she stopped caring. If they were real, so be it. If not, that was fine also. A little disconcerting, but maybe they were trying to help her or just be a part of her life. Was she an unwilling sacrifice? An assistant to this imaginary magician?

She lived several lives at night, while Leon and everyone else slept. Each story, like a memory, seemed to take a little bit of her away with it. She didn't care if the movie studio called because she had her own private moving pictures.

She wished she could sleep and enter the darkness with her own dreams. Maybe that was all these movies without movie stars were, her own dreams writhing before her. She watched Leon's sculpted, smooth face as he dreamed, grimaces, contortions, smiles, his eyelids twitching like flies. She tried to guess what he saw: sun warming the dew on cold grass; sky sutured with clouds; sex; some event that was wonderful or terrible.

Once Leon woke to find Lil blinking at him from a chair,

a slippered foot hidden under the bed, her painted fingernails snaking along the bed covers. She was drawing close to
interpret his body. But when his eyes were open he couldn't
remember his dreams anymore. Instead he drew her close,
felt her soft fingers reaching around him, her dark hair blan-
keting his chest. Her bottom lip was split and swollen. He
didn't know why or what had happened to her during the
night. He ran a finger over her sore lip but she didn't flinch.
He wanted to bring both himself and Lil fully back into the
world together.

"Vaudeville's dying and I won't be sad to see it go." Izzy
sipped coffee, adjusted her yellow turban hat over her curly
hair. Her legs were crossed and her black and white shoes
darted back and forth. She had a big, lovely smile. "Now
jazz, that's the thing. Brings in the customers more than that
blackface stuff." She'd noticed more people drunkenly falling off their chairs lately. More than usual, but they were
replaced soon enough.

Leon looked around the club Izzy would sing at that
night. A man was wiping down the bar. It was empty except
for Izzy and Leon. All the other chairs sat upside down on
tables, their legs pointed into the air. A Victrola played quietly. Leon was all for having fun, as much as an accountant
could. "How's Marco?" he asked.

"Good. His fingers have been flying over the piano keys
lately." Her smile overtook her mouth, ran away with it.
Sometimes, when she was nervous or scared, she thought of
her audience as plants, strange, creeping foliage. At that mo-

ment Leon seemed to be an odd leafy plant, growing side-
ways, toward the sun. "But we're here to talk about Lil and
the way she's been acting lately. I've noticed her doing some
screwy things and I wanted to talk to you about them."

"Yes," he said. "I've been concerned about her too."

"She stopped by my dressing room last week and asked
to borrow the gloves I had been wearing in my show. When
I gave them to her, she put them on and began running her
hands up and down my door like she was inspecting it. Next
she pulled them off and gave them back to me. 'They're use-
less,' she said. When I asked her what she was doing, she
said, 'An experiment.'"

"I found her talking to a closet a few days ago." Leon
looked downcast. His blonde hair was dark in the dim light;
his eyes paced the length of the newly cleaned bar. "She was
asking it where the sailor was hiding."

"I assume the closet didn't answer her."

"A few nights ago she threw all her knives and forks on
the kitchen floor for no reason. She told me 'to take them all
away' and 'to go dry up' because the floor was turning to
water and she wanted to float away on it in peace." Leon's
face thickened with shadows. He remembered the piercing
sound of the silverware, which made him think of the startling yellow color of Izzy's hat. He had immediately thrown
away every sharp object in Lil's apartment.

"What should we do?"

"I don't know. What can we do?"

"She doesn't seem harmful to herself or anyone else,
does she?"

"I don't think so. I don't really know." Leon wondered

what she could learn from the things she did. What was
wrong with her? Could he help?

"You know how she feels about George?" Izzy asked.

"Yes."

"Then why do you stay with her?"

Leon could hear her breathing in the silence that followed. "I think I wanted her to rescue me." He laughed a
little, realizing how ridiculous that sounded.

"From what?" She stirred her coffee with a spoon, looked
at him.

"From an accountant's life." From more than that, but
he hadn't really put it into words before. Now he had seen
what a hero's life really was like, and he didn't want it. He
had to admit that he actually did like numbers. He didn't
understand art, what made it good or not good. There was
only what he liked or didn't like, and he was unsure of that.
He watched Izzy's swirl of brown and ochre topped by the
bright yellow hat. She looked serious. "Little did I know that
I'd be the one to do all the rescuing."

She nodded.

"So why does she stay with me?"

"Because she can't have George right now." She rolled
up a sleeve on her dress. "I'm not sure anyone can."

Leon felt relieved to confess. Izzy sat straight-backed, elegant, her voice far away, drifting closer. Her tall, vase-like
body soothed him.

"Right now," he said wearily, "I just want to know what's
troubling her and making her seem so crazy." Lil was certainly an unwilling sacrifice and there was no admiration
involved in her situation.

"Oh," Izzy was smiling, "I'm concerned for her, but I don't think we need to tell anyone else about her troubles, especially if they don't notice anything, like her patrons, the Beckers. And I think I might know three or four people who could be more off their nuts than Lil."

"I'm confused and I can only go one way or the other," Lil said. "I either want to fuck the whole world, including you, Dr. Duncan, or else I'm completely paralyzed and I want to do nothing." She laughed. "I must represent the times." If she was noisy and defiant, she hoped no one would notice all the changes in her. Lil's dark bob swung around her head. She imitated her old self. She thought about whatever sentences she used to say and then she said them. She hadn't had to consider them before.

In order to be rescued, you'd need to be in danger, she thought. Or want to be. She wanted the responsibility for her own life. She didn't want to have to thank or blame anyone. That way she'd never be hurt.

"Maybe your paralysis is merely a time of questioning." His fingers formed the shape of a pyramid that was empty inside. Devoid of any treasures or mummies, his hands covered other people's pasts, patted them down, reshaped them.

"Are you saying that I should stick only to the action, the fucking?" She liked to argue with him as though he were a movie director giving her instructions. Except that Dr. Duncan was never very explicit.

"No, of course not. Let's try another method." Dr. Dun-

can's long fingers removed four objects from his drawer. "Now describe each of these."

Lil stood. She wanted to tell him that when she felt imprisoned was when she wanted to fuck the most. Right then she was imprisoned by her own body, her own mind. Herself. But instead he wanted her to play this game. She was composed. She rolled his apple in her palms. "Red and round. Hmm, what does that remind me of?" She raised her finger. "Besides Adam and Eve?" She rubbed the apple along the front of her dress just as Baby Chapman would have done. She could feel the contours with it, the bumps and buttons on her dress. She put the apple down and looked at him with her large, brown eyes. She picked up the newspaper he held out for her. Unfolding it, she said, "It can't tell me what I want to know."

"And what's that?"

"The future, not the past." Why couldn't it divulge the cure to what was happening to her? At least there weren't any more articles about Leon. She popped the monocle that hung from a chain around her neck onto her right eye. She squinted and held it in place. "For example, here's an article about Clarence Darrow and Leopold and Loeb. Must we know why they did it? Couldn't they have killed for no reason? Maybe it was just a thought that passed through their heads and somehow became real for a day or a few days and they didn't even know that they acted on it."

Dr. Duncan made a noise like a murmur and wrote something down. "Does that ever happen to you, Miss Moore?"

Lil stared at the newspaper. For a moment she wondered whether she should tell him about her private moving pictures. He already knew too much about her. He would most likely have to do something about them. She could end up in an asylum. "No, I only act after I've thought about it." But she knew she was impulsive, knocking the top hats off of stage door Johnnies or tripping sugar daddies that her mother dated when Lil was a young girl. Now, it was just things for fun, too much hooch or glad rags or too many men.

Dr. Duncan noticed a change in Lil. She had become more careful about what she said and did. As though she was rehearsing. She didn't pass through the boundaries of her memories again, didn't return to the important incidents. "Have you always done that?"

"No." She thought of the girl she used to be in braids stiff as paintbrushes, of the soft, over-washed sweater she wore, even to sleep. Had she once been like Alice, using her clothes as skin? Were her long, thin arms wrapped around herself at night as consolation while her mother screamed out in pleasure with her boyfriend? She believed he might kill her, or was he in the act of killing her? Was Lil's pleasure like that? Sudden, unplanned, as noisy as death. Was she becoming her mother?

There was silence while Dr. Duncan wished she would do more with the newspaper, pick out articles that interested her, which they could discuss. He could see what she chose, try to understand why and how that choice illuminated her illness. But to his disappointment, she put the newspaper aside. It rustled as she threw it in a loose ball onto his desk.

Chef Puts Cheese on Hamburger

Last week Lionel Steinberger, chef of The Rite Spot in Pasadena, California, created the first cheeseburger...

The rest of the story was rumpled. He would have to write up the sequence of her actions, for that told him her priorities, the sexual, intellectual, emotional, and whatever came next. He would watch for psychosis or for schizophrenia since they could remain hidden for only so long.

Lil said, "I see the sun, but there are hidden storm clouds, at your window." Dr. Duncan wrote that down too. So she decided not to use any more words. She took the pencil and the blank piece of paper from his desk and drew a caricature of the doctor with simple, unsteady black lines. His nose was too big, his eyes desperate, his white suit too large and fluid. She gave him the sketch.

"Thank you, Lil." He hardly looked at it, placing it into the drawer with his other objects.

She realized that the sketch was more art than she'd done in the last few weeks. There was no one to save her. Dr. Duncan was a Pharaoh, already buried with his life's objects, categorizing them, reinterpreting their meaning, thereby avoiding life itself. He could ask me what I have left unfinished and catalogue that too, she decided. Her mother had once said dreamily to Lil, as she looked at a daguerreotype of her own mother, "Imagine becoming a memory." As if it was something wonderful.

Lil arranged the apple, the abandoned pen, and the crumpled newspaper on his desk into a still life. She took off her monocle so she didn't need to squint. She put the monocle next to the apple with its happy shade of red. She stood back and gazed at her efforts, wondering what the old Lil would do. She thought of a poem Marco had quoted, "In every accident there is the victim,/ lingering like perfume after an encounter." She decided that she didn't like these things enough to draw them. At least that would have been how the old Lil felt, so she would pretend that was how she felt also.

"I could have written messages on that paper," she finally said.

"You could have done an infinite number of things."

"I could have said: *Help! I'm being held in a psychiatrist's office as a prisoner until I improve.* Then I could have tossed it out the window."

He glanced at his watch, straightened his white suit. "Your time is up."

"I'm not going back to Mrs. Becker's psychiatrist," Lil told the first man whose wrist she grabbed at the speakeasy. He had a robust, pink-cheeked face that fixed on several girls with large blackened eyes walking by in a group.

"Good for you, girlie," he said, not even looking her way, his eyes following the girls. He disentangled himself from her grip and moved toward them. "Twenty-three skidoo."

"What about me?" Leon asked on the telephone after she thanked him for the tulips he had sent her. She told him that she didn't want to see Dr. Duncan anymore.

"What about you?" She paused, her voice growing deeper and rougher. "I don't know."

"Still?" There was so much disappointment in his voice.

Lil tried to explain to Leon that if she opened a tube of paint she didn't want it to go to waste. She wasn't sure that what she was saying came out correctly. But it was the same with Leon. She told him a body had few boundaries and that ultimately it didn't really matter.

She knew she had upset him. "I'm sorry," she said, "I don't know if art will even exist in the future."

She put on a dazzling pink sweater and a coat over her nightdress and a pair of good shoes. She wandered between Forty-seventh and Forty-ninth streets on Fifth Avenue. She watched who left the buildings and quickly decided on one she was fairly certain was a juice joint. She poured herself into a group of young men and women lingering outside. One woman in a flapper dress said to Lil, "You look like the cat's pajamas." It fit too well. Lil laughed and returned, "Then you must be the bee's knees." She heard a man from her crowd say to the peephole, "Joe sent me." And they all went in at once.

She wanted at least one drink. It was crowded, yet a few couples had made enough room on the floor to dance the Charleston and the Camel Walk. She ordered a gin at the bar, shouting at the distant, busy bartender, and a line of three people passed the glass to her.

"Bananas! Bananas for sale," a woman in a poke hat and a drab, sepia-colored dress called out. A tray in her hands was half filled with long, yellow bananas. They were a novelty. "Ten cents each," she yelled above the din.

Lil sat away from the hubbub, tired, her hand gathered

along the back of an empty chair she found near a wall. A woman with black hair pulled into a large comb sat next to her doing a crossword puzzle under the dim light. Lil thought of the Beckers and their money and wondered what party they were at—was it one of their own? Many smiling faces passed her by. Lil rose to buy a bottle and she asked the black-haired woman to save her chair. When she returned, an older man sat in the woman's chair and a thin couple wearing satin was necking in her chair. She wished she could be at home, painting, trying to sleep, or spooning with Leon, if he would let her now. But she wanted to avoid her visions, wanted to forget her own personal moving pictures.

For a moment Lil believed she saw Mary Beach, her red hair flying out from a cloche hat, a diamond brooch fixed to her blouse, talking to a handsome gangster who was holding a deck of playing cards. A smiling Beatrice looked up at them both lovingly. Then Mary and Beatrice disappeared and the woman selling bananas took their place. Lil spied several women carrying banana trays, for the woman had split into two, and then three versions of herself. It didn't matter whether she was at home or not, she couldn't stop the visions, but she did feel better among a group of people.

Lil lit a cigarette, gulped from her gin bottle. She wanted to distract herself. I'm pink, she realized. I'm the color pink. It's a color that can bud from trees, yet doesn't lose its distinction. It covers our mouths, inside and out, coats our organs, our genitals. It's for girls. The mixing of red and white. It lines out the highways and major roads on maps. It lives in the bathroom, in sinks and bathtubs. And it's shocking on a bridge or building or car. A color for contingencies, for when red has faded or icy white has been defiled by red.

Lil's dark eyes were bleary, her coat slipped off her shoulders. It was like one of the Beckers' parties except that she didn't know anyone and didn't care to. She'd been to speakeasies before, but she never returned to the same one again. They all seemed the same. The drinking, the smoking, some dancing, some kissing, the vanishing, and the lively people that newly arrived. Disappearing was the point, but first came all the usual amusements. A man smiled at her with gaps in his teeth and said, "You're some good-looking doll." She could imagine the force of his whispers, how his words would stutter. The room boiled.

Suddenly a whistle blew loudly and clearly. Time stood still for a moment. From the malicious shadows along a wall Lil believed she saw her mother. She waved in Lil's direction although her neck was bent into an odd angle. Lil could see that her feet didn't quite touch the ground. The whistle began again. Time returned. The bartender pressed a button and several drop-shelves pushed the liquor bottles into hidden compartments. He hit a switch and some of the lights went out. Everyone ran for the door, taking Lil with them, trampling Lil's tossed cigarette. At the door someone shouted, "It's a staged raid. We can go back inside." Lil saw the rush back into the room, but she remained outside. People hurried inside again and, as people passed her, Lil noticed a red scarf, the smell of something sour and harsh like vinegar, painted bird earrings, someone upchucking onto the sidewalk, a silk tie with stains, someone jangling keys, gold cuff links with diamonds, a young boy in a suit too small for him. A woman with indigo lips walked by her and, laughing, turned back to the gin mill. Lil stayed outside.

Lil heard the faint nocturne of a piano player in the cold, crisp night. Stars gleamed wetly and watched the unapologetic moon in the dark sky. She could feel air struggling with her coat and goosebumps raised the hair along her arms beneath her sleeves. She thought about navigating by the seasons. How spring would come, although it was hard to believe. There was still Christmas and New Year's to anticipate, and she grew tired. A chilly metal Cadillac moved slowly along the street. A young girl with large eyes stared at Lil, at the erupting noise and lights beginning again in the space behind Lil. A man wearing a heavy coat and a hat tipped low over his face briskly strode by, then stopped a few feet away.

"Are you lost? Do you need some help, honey?" the man's mouth asked.

"No," she said, feeling smaller than usual. And yes, she was actually lost among the city's buildings and streets and people, needing more help than anyone could give. She didn't know how to stop what was happening to her. She didn't know whom to tell, whom she could trust. She could feel the sharp pulse of the wind along her body like too many knives. "No, I'm going home." She shifted toward the cold, invisible breath that would taunt her all the way home.

~

Female Troubles?

"I Felt Lots Better After Taking W.E. Redfern's Vegetable Compound."

Westward, Wisconsin. "I took W.E. Redfern's Vegetable Compound after my son was born because two of my sisters recommended it. I was in agonizing pain and in bed. But after taking four bottles, I got up and have been taking care of my son ever since." —Mrs. Estelle Grant

There are many stories like this one of new mothers left weakened and in a run-down condition and for whom caring for their baby is well-nigh impossible. W.E. Redfern's Vegetable Compound is a tonic for the mother both before and after childbirth and is beneficial to the entire system. Weak and inflamed nerves respond rapidly. Prepared with medicinal roots and herbs, it can be taken safely by nursing mothers.

Virginia City, Nevada. "Female complaints? Ulceration, Ovarian troubles, Inflammation? I suffered them all. W.E. Redfern's Vegetable Compound cured them completely. It Dissolves Tumors, fixes Indigestion, Nervous Prostration, Bloating, General Disability. It acts in harmony with the governing laws of the female system. I don't know what I would do without it." – Lydia Rivers

Try W.E. Redfern's Vegetable Compound to fix all your female complaints.

For sale by druggists everywhere.

~

Instead of trying to paint, Lil lay on her bed. She remembered her past, desolation disguised as intimacy, intimacy disguised as fun and games, the fun and games a way of forgetting, and pretending that they were meaningless. It was a big circle of memory. So what if she lost her memory? Would that be so bad? She traced the tributaries of her fingers, followed the lines mapping her palm. She knew this hand. It had caressed skin, arranged flowers in a still life, smoked too many cigarettes, and revised her paintings. She would always recognize it, wouldn't she?

She berated Leon's white and yellow tulips drooping in a vase. "Why don't you leave me alone?" After art and George, Leon was left, lurking, hanging on to her. Always there, reassuring in a way she wasn't used to. She plucked a yellow tulip and placed it behind her left ear. It was what she'd heard women did on the Tahitian islands to show that they were available.

Lil decided to take a bath. She ran the taps. When she sank into the soapy water, with her chin submerged and her feet resting on the white porcelain, she saw two tiny hands flickering across from her on the bathroom wall. Small as her fingernails, they were webs of a fluttering light. They were little waving fists. She closed her eyes and opened them again. Grimaces shifted, gaudy and violent as clouds. She saw two bent legs, with folding flesh, pounding a ghostly table. Silent crying. Hair so sparse it seemed to dissolve.

Lil cried and her tears rained onto the bath water. She scraped her knuckles as she reached to hold the baby boy. Coins of water littered the floor. He continued his crying and kicking. She had once asked a neighbor wearing a thin, flowered bathrobe who was retrieving her newspaper if she saw the monstrous man against the wall. "No," the woman sighed, "and I hope I never will." The woman's face full of fear below her plucked eyebrows as she hurried to lock her door.

Lil had named the baby Horace, so he wouldn't get into any kind of trouble. This baby who had been smothered within her own flesh. She had become angry and tired of

her own body and hurt herself with what was nearby, a palette knife. Then, as suddenly as it had appeared, the baby
disappeared and left a blank, white wall. This baby who had
never breathed air and was never mentioned to anyone.

George's baby.

Two days before the exhibition, Alice was tidying up at the
gallery because Mary Beach was gone for good and there
wasn't anyone else to help. Alice was thinking about the
people that had bought her paintings while she whisked a
feather duster around the bronze statue of a naked man's
torso twisted toward the front door. She was mindlessly
dusting his back and buttocks over and over again. One
woman patron told Alice that she liked women artists because women thought alike, and then the woman tried to
bargain Alice down in price. "Then could I give you a piece
of jewelry in exchange for the painting?" she asked Alice's
shaking head. One couple told her that they liked her painting of a large mango cut crosswise and viewed from above
because it reminded them of a pet they had owned that was
hit by an automobile. An older, natty-looking man told her
that her art was "mysterious, sexual, a catalyst for discovery,
an experience that cannot be distilled" as he blew cigarette
smoke down her loose shirt. For two months afterwards he
didn't pick up the painting he bought from the gallery, saying first that he had gone on vacation and then that he was
busy. Alice decided that she would attend the exhibition
(since she had to) but not go to the Beckers' party at their
country house afterwards.

Alice liked the gallery but would rather be painting ripe fruit, split open to show its intricate interior. She studied other people's work, Rodin, Matisse, Cezanne, and wondered if she was becoming her subject: pulpy, wet fruit, contained by its rind. It was just that George needed her help for the show. She felt dreamy at the gallery, with its window-sized paintings, all openings to other lives and landscapes.

Canvases were hung from the ceiling to the floor. Many were portraits, so people she didn't know watched her, peeking from the different frames. There were landscapes, several still lifes, groups and figures, and Alice's own obsession, fruit. They stared at her from the paintings as if they were waiting for something or someone. Others were going about their business or gazing off into the room. It was a women's exhibition including Alice, Lil, Marguerite Zorach, and Rebecca ("Beck") Salsbury, the daughter of Nate Salsbury, the flamboyant manager of Buffalo Bill's Wild West Show. Many of Beck's paintings showed cowboys and Indians in repose, on their days off, playing cards. Marguerite Zorach's *Nude Reclining* showed a woman who was all horizon and acceptance in a sunny room splintered with succulent plants, blowsy curtains, and opaque windows. Windows upon windows, on into the imagination. A modern woman's mind. Four stone sculptures on tables depicted childbirth in abstract curves and indentations. Alice's feather duster sat still on the bronze man's knees. Lil had several landscapes and one portrait, of the gone Mary Beach, called *Bougainvillea*. It was large and startling with its wild colors and brushstrokes.

Alice smelled cigarette smoke first and then Lil entered

the room. The odor lingered on Lil's clothes, the coat and
the playful dress shaped like a corset. Alice pulled at the
scalloped edge of her old sweater and held the duster at her
side. She brushed back her stray hair and jutted her pointy
chin out toward Lil. Lil took up all the space in a room.

"So this is the essence of women painters in 1924," Lil
said, rotating around. She studied the interiors of other
rooms, bodies, faces, landscapes. Gender showed in the gestures, in the subject matter: children, a house, the turning of
a cheek. Things were changing but Lil still felt suffocated,
especially because there were barely enough women for the
exhibit. "What about for 1925?" she inquired.

"Maybe George will do an exhibit by female children
who are painters since he's always looking for something
different."

"Both of them?" Lil smiled. "How about an exhibit of
chickens? Paintings that have chickens in them. Portraits,
odalisques, still lifes and sculptures with eggs." Lil had an
impulse to prance and squawk, scrape her toes on the floor.
But she didn't. She considered the chicken's small lives with
their small wrongs. How commendable in a way. They both
laughed, although they both saw the betrayal, knowing that
George was one of those men who adored women.

Lil had come to offer George her irretrievable heart, hoping no one else would be around. It was time. She couldn't
live posthumously. Her day had gone badly already, a thin
wind, deceptive streets, shifting street lamps, too many
ghosts. The sky was something eaten and spit out onto the
sidewalk. She cursed all the way there, but her words were
swept away, over cars and scarves and an aching light. She

had wanted to mimic pigeons with their nodding heads and silly, splayed feet, the way they scavenged for anything resembling food. It was a day of birds: chickens, sparrows, pigeons, and her voice like a crow's. Birds were lucky, flying away, leaving everything behind. They followed their migratory hearts as they reached into the sky. Everything on the earth would grow tiny as they navigated through stray clouds and disappeared.

"How's married life?"

Alice looked steadily at the gleaming wooden floor of the gallery. "Fine." Had she actually said it? But their lives had been geared toward the exhibition lately. She also wondered if George was having an affair with a dancer he had met at the Beckers', or a married French woman. The older French woman had seemed squalid in furs and diamonds as she sauntered through the gallery a few weeks ago, buying three paintings with three successive sweeps of her hand.

Lil rummaged in her embroidered pocketbook, her hair forming a dark crescent along her cheek. Her hand came out empty. "Oh, my goodness," she said, "I've just run out of cigarettes." The darting, repeatable birds she had seen earlier on the street came to mind, the actions they did over and over again to survive, how they all looked the same to Lil. The same bird in her path became a flock, or else she was seeing things again. One bird exaggerated into four, a Cubist bird. At least they had the sense to fly somewhere else for the winter.

"Please don't smoke in here. George doesn't like it," Alice said, towering over Lil.

"I know. I need to talk to George about my paintings and

then I'll leave. I'm so desperate for a cigarette already. Could you go out and get me some? I promise I'll smoke it when I leave. I just want to have it now, in my fingers." It was an excuse. It was a small price to pay to get George alone.

"Yes, I'll get my coat and go." The feather duster was abandoned by the statues.

When Lil's shoes clicked into the back room behind him, George turned around, bent down, kissed her forehead. She closed her eyes. He was fussing with a frame. Paint and small knives, a hammer and wire surrounded him. He clutched the piece of wood and frowned and yet seemed buoyant and entertained by his work. Lil could watch his hands for hours.

"The show should be swell," he said.

"It'll be one of your best." She watched his mustache and she smiled, looking up toward him. "Alice went out for cigarettes."

"Why? She doesn't smoke." His back was toward her again.

"For me." She wanted one now, to watch smoke etching the air, to do something with her mouth and hands. The gallery was silent now and she was disquieted. She wanted to have conversations with the art, discussing her ideas. First she had to absorb the picture, let it speak. "My paintings look good."

"You're pleased with their placement and the whole idea of the show?" He thought of Alice, uncomfortable purchasing cigarettes, her feet shuffling, her shy manner. Her bones cracking, as they did every morning when she awakened, her skeleton shrinking. This morning he had been thinking of excuses for coming home late the night before.

"Yes." Her fingers found his collar, followed its outline. He removed her hand without turning toward her or looking at her. "It's time soon," she said.

"For what?" He sawed a picture frame in front of him, which made a grating sound.

"To go away together." She looked at her shoes but imagined a warm place with a terrace and philodendrons, a sun the color of blood. The boat docked below them, bobbing in vacant blue water. Half-finished paintings festered by the warm windows. George.

George faced her, his eyes flashed, his face furious, his gray mustache moving above his lips. "You have to understand that I'm married now. What was between us was over long ago. You're a good painter, Lil, with a promising future, and I'm sure we'll sell your paintings at the show. Use the money for a vacation. You're young. Take a rest, have a good time somewhere. Take Leon with you." He held her hand and patted it. He was composed. He could hear the front door opening and closing and Alice's sweet, uncertain steps into the large room. "But now you must leave me alone."

Lil turned from him, hurt yet unbelieving. He would be her undoing, not her savior. She had never heard of him pushing away a lover before. They often hung about the periphery of his life, changing in relation to new events and people. If he took a trip out West, a woman he had known years ago would arrive at his hotel room or at a party, an old love would appear from behind a door. They were everywhere, it seemed, and he never pushed them away.

She had never seen him so stern, except with his daugh-

ter. Lil wanted him, had dreamed of having him all to herself. Yet her mouth felt blistered, her eyes welled with tears
as turpentine sometimes stung them that way. She thought
of the postcards she wouldn't send now. Ones that said,
"Sun is a remedy. George and I have finally happened. And
the boat just carried us away (ha, ha)." She wouldn't have
wanted to see Alice's or Leon's faces. Maybe George meant
for her to leave him alone until after the show. She felt suddenly better, not so wounded. That must have been what he
meant, that she should leave him alone until after the show
and then they could be together again. She brushed wetness
from her lower eyelashes. She would speak to the George
she saw at her apartment, one of the multiple Georges. He
promised her so many wonderful things.

Her shoes tapped into the gallery where she evaluated
the paintings' duplicity along with images sprung from the
artists' minds. Just like her strange visions. Alice looked
shaggy in her too-large sweater, a skirt that hung below
her knees and socks. She was a sad creature amid the color
splashed onto the walls, the heartfelt canvases. She held out
the newly purchased pack of cigarettes.

"Thanks," Lil said, tearing the packet from Alice's hands
and rushing out the door.

Leon had numbers. They gathered underneath his desk
lamp on the rectangular papers. They were penned on napkins at lunches with clients. He arranged them and they
spoke to him, telling him about someone's past, present,
and future. If he had lived in ancient Egypt he would have

been buried with them. They were his art. Sometimes they entered his dreams, a large nine suspended in the air or a human-sized five chasing him down some stairs. In harsh whispers, they said, "You need us," and laughed.

He loved them fiercely, red and black, silent, all the equations, equivalents, tabulations. They embodied the rock-bottom truth. He might have saved George if the other party, the collector, had been more willing to negotiate, if Leon had liked George more and pushed harder. If George had come to him early on, maybe he could have reshuffled the numbers, bent them more to George's advantage. Leon tipped his desk lamp closer to the raw figures of an older gentleman who had been trying to start a jewelry business, one financed by mob money. The calculations returned to their sources, like rivers to the ocean. Papers sprouted from his desk drawers.

Alma entered, bringing the smell of her flowery perfume, and placed some sharpened pencils on Leon's desk. She bit her lips, which reminded him of fruit. Some days Leon liked being alone with his numbers. They were capable of endearments and surprises. They had their standard shapes and sizes, but they could still be sad or tell a good joke. And, like the Egyptian hieroglyphics, his work would outlast him.

Leon pulled on his coat. The sky was darkening. A dog barked at him as he made his way through the bundled crowds of people toward his favorite luncheonette. He sat at the counter and ordered a coffee, black, and a cheese sandwich. "The usual, for the good-looking piker over here," the waitress, whose hands had large, brown spots, yelled to the cook as she was pouring coffee into Leon's white cup with cracks along the sides. A woman sat next to him, wearing a tight dress with a leopard-spotted collar and a large, round hat. She was leaving prints from her pink lips on an identical cup of coffee. Something in Leon stirred. He wondered what it was he needed from Lil to feel better, to feel complete, to finish.

"Leopold and Loeb just got life in prison," Leon said to the woman on the counter seat next to him. He passed her the sugar. He found himself staring at her blue eyes and straw-colored hair. Her pinky stood straight out as she sipped her coffee. The luncheonette letters on the window formed long shadows across the counter and along the floor.

"It was a passing entertainment." She didn't smile or blink. Her lipstick blossomed along the edge of the cup. One foot with a stiletto heel tapped under the counter. Her shoes were lemon-colored. Light from the circle of metal on the dinette seat she sat on bothered Leon's eyes. He shaded them.

He estimated the cost of her outfit and the expenses involved in keeping a woman like her happy. It was more than he could afford. "Do you mean that people will find another event or trial amusing soon enough?"

"No," and she smoothed a pair of yellow gloves on her lap. "I mean the murder itself. To Leopold and Loeb. It was simply a passing form of entertainment, a way to spend their time. Just like listening to music or reading a book. Now they'll have to spend their time in prison."

"Nice talking to you," Leon said, abruptly getting up. "I need to get back to my office." She disgusted him. He sensed that she was also seeking a passing form of entertainment. He left hurriedly; she was an incorrect sum.

Pentimento

Leon was glad he wasn't famous anymore. No one sent over food at the Chinese restaurant. Since his rescue there had been several people who had helped in automobile accidents, one man who had dragged two children from a flaming car, several speakeasy raids, three salesmen dead indirectly from the Florida real estate boom, a few gangsters pumped with gunfire and a ten-year-old girl hit by a stray bullet outside a restaurant. All had been documented in the newspapers in the last three weeks. He was forgotten. No more flowers with kind notes, or kisses from girls who had seen his picture in the papers. The world moved on, finding the new. Which left numbers for Leon to harness, explain, and make usable.

Leon noticed four empty chairs with plates of food in various stages of congealment on the round, white table-cloth. Napkins had words scribbled on them and were tufted like teepees or stuffed into empty water glasses. Three forks were arranged to form the letter F. Leon had come too late, missing the writers again.

"Fitzgerald was here," Marco said, confirming Leon's suspicions. He smiled and his gold tooth sparkled like the promise of another era. "He was carrying Zelda. They'd been to a play where he had tried to take off all his clothes at the end and the audience, as well as the staff, stopped him."

Izzy looked at Marco and then Leon. "He folded Zelda into a chair like an overcoat." Izzy wore an indigo evening dress. An explosion of yellow lilies, another gift, sat next to her on an empty seat.

"It's nice to know that there are people more untamed than me." Lil's smoke exited through her nose and wafted over her empty white plate.

"Apparently Zelda's mother had been in a sanitarium," Alice said softly, rubbing the crook of her arm so her loose sweater sleeve slipped up and down.

"I've heard they're overrated." Lil inhaled and looked at the litter of dishes on the table and the waiters talking excitedly near the kitchen, their hands continuing the conversation.

Lil reached for a cup of tea and her fingers missed the rim by a few inches. She couldn't stand a place where people's screams and shouting wouldn't let a person think. There were all those activities for patients that were supposed to take the place of art. And the things that they did to you there. She knew Leopold and Loeb could be there, or in jail, for an act for which there was no explanation. Like life. Art's only reason for existence was the beauty of the expression. The grace and what it said to someone. "I need my eyes checked."

Izzy rose from her chair and sang for her supper. Her curly hair bouncing, her wide nose widening, her white teeth flashing. No one knew why she decided to sing just then. She sang, "Everybody loves my baby (but my baby don't love nobody but me)." She sang loudly and without music. When she was done, two diners at another table sent over rice and noodles. Everyone in the restaurant clapped.

"Every so often I feel the need to do that," was all she said. Marco stood, his black hair slicked back, his gold tooth refracting light. He was delighted by her get-up-and-go. He hoped she wouldn't throw him over soon. She was magnificent, a wonderful singer. They could play music together for a long time.

"What do the rest of us have to eat?" Leon asked, noticing that George was quiet, withdrawn, his gray mustache curled into his upper lip. He appeared to be uncomfortable. Leon began to eat along with Izzy.

Alice's hand braceleted George's wrist. She wouldn't mind living in a museum, the quiet, the inspiration, nothing to do but observe and paint, but George created turmoil, knocking over a plum that she had set up yesterday morning in a still life on top of a table. The boat in Long Island had gently tipped and then George grew angry at her. "Why did you put it there? You're always placing something in other people's way and then we can't help but knock it down and destroy whatever it is by mistake." He turned away and then he turned back again. "It's just something to eat, just a plum." But he knew better. He felt wrong and riddled with guilt. He stomped out and Alice didn't know where he went.

She sat on the built-in sofa, watching the continuous clouds, the beckoning water, the sky that opened up, but later was overcome by darkness. George came home the next day, just before they were supposed to go to the New York Chinese restaurant. Alice's stomach felt like a bonfire and her heart felt coughed up, like something left on a sidewalk. But she was growing accustomed to his difficult behavior.

She was learning to ignore his silly utterances and gestures when he was there, which was becoming a rarity. She didn't really care where he went. She only hoped that he would be happier there.

"Alice is working on a series about plums," George announced gloomily. Her art was saleable and would outlast them all. He hated to interfere with her work, since she was remarkable with or without him. People had begun to ask at the gallery to see her paintings, and they asked if she was doing any more. One woman with an eight-year-old girl had looked at a painting with thick, ripe bananas and the little girl had reached for the fruit.

Lil had liked Fitzgerald when she met him and Zelda at the restaurant that night. It was immediately after Sherwood Anderson and Jean Toomer had left, saying, "You're welcome to take off your clothes here, F. Scott, but only after we've gone." Fitzgerald removed his jacket, his vest, and his tie. He carefully placed his wristwatch in the center of the round table. Zelda, her hair waved, was crumpled in a chair, quiet, her eyes closed.

"Sometimes the only salvation is extravagance," Fitzgerald, stripped down to his pants and shirt, whispered to Lil, the prettiest, youngest artist at the table. Then he ate all of the fried rice.

"Why not?" Zelda proclaimed and drifted back into her stupor.

"Art is a romance that saves us," Lil responded. "At least that's what Dr. Duncan, my former psychoanalyst, said." She rolled her eyes. Alice looked at her and they laughed.

"I love fairy tales," George piped up. "I used to read

them to my daughter."

"Everyone loves a happy ending." Leon had finished eating, his angular face content, his blonde hair darker under the dim light. He still wanted to put his arm around Lil, although she was growing distant and distracted. Strange how she wanted gin for breakfast, forgetting what time it was. She hadn't touched him in a while. He wasn't sure why he kept trying.

Lil saw abstract lines in the glasses on the table. The conjunction between space and objects was becoming blurred. Things were merging with the air and into each other. It was getting harder for everything to keep its shape, to maintain its distinction. Everything became a nuance, a gradation. All composition and perspective were possible. There was chiaroscuro, light and dark. All moving or still pictures, but pictures nonetheless. It was getting harder to tell what was real and what wasn't.

Sounds echoed, as though Lil lived in a seashell. Voices grew deeper and journeyed down a tunnel and then returned. They had generous, important tones except that afterwards she heard a ringing, as if her ears couldn't bear their absence. Some nights Lil longed for pure silence, although now she could hear her own blood coursing through her veins. She heard the pulse of it like too much paint freshly squeezed from a tube.

"Art must learn how to swim then," George added, winking at Leon, the master swimmer and hero. "We can see if the unsold paintings can do the crawl or the backstroke after the show."

"What does writing know how to do then?" Lil turned

her spoon over, her face elongated strangely in the concave curve. She moved it and she became too wide and round. It was disturbing. "Tap dance?"

"Yes." Izzy cleared her throat. "What about music and songs?"

"That's easy," Marco ran his finger along Izzy's shoulder. "Music knows how to smoke a cigarette and drink giggle water."

They all laughed except for Leon. He could total the bill for the evening in a few minutes in his head if only he knew what everyone had eaten.

~

The Roving Reporter
Every Day He Asks Three Random People a Question

The Question: Do you think that film producer Thomas Ince died of a heart attack aboard William Randolph Hearst's boat, the *Oneida*?

Miss Gertrude Blackwell, clerk – No. From what I've heard Hearst shot Ince in a jealous fit over Marion Davies, the film actress. And they say that Charlie Chaplin and columnist Luella Parsons were there too.

Henry Keating, real estate – I say no. Hearst probably shot him by accident. It was during the producer's 42nd birthday party and you know how these things can happen.

Lillian Moore, painter – William Blake wrote, "Exuberance is beauty."

~

"Lemme see that one again," the man yelled at the projectionist behind the glass window. The heavy, balding producer sat in an empty motion picture room at the Hollywood studio. He puffed on a cigar and smoke surrendered to the beam of light focused on the screen. His brown suit already smelled like the cigar. He was thinking about the rushes for a new picture called "What She Did" with a Valentino look-alike who pranced across the stage and sang lullabies to wide-eyed women. It seemed to delight audiences, especially the women. It was amazing what you could convince women of with mere perseverance, hope, and general good looks. He picked up the glass of bourbon at his feet with his free hand and peered deeply into its swirling abyss. He liked the new bootlegger, a Mr. Ocean or Mr. Lake or Mr. Waves or something like that. That man knew his business and carried good liquor as well as doing him other unnamable favors. Mr. Something was from New York but he came out West regularly.

The reel was ready and started up again. In black and white, darkness and light, "Lil", her real name was Lillian Moore, held up a mirror, smiled, and talked to someone off screen. She made a face of mock horror, her arms thrown into the air, her features pulled upwards as though by the wind. She asked for directions from someone behind the camera. Next she melted onto a chair, her arms folded and her face saddened, her eyes cast down.

The man could see that she was short when she stood next to the chair. That was fine, many of the leading men were shorter than they appeared on screen. Like Charlie Chaplin. But her happy face was too frenetic, too forced. Her eyebrows flew upward, her mouth began its episodic flight, her chin jutted and shook. Yet her eyes blazed and seemed to fill with obscene afterthoughts. She could shatter a man. She was very appealing. He watched her carefully as she asked for instructions. Acting naturally, she resembled Theda Bara. Lillian Moore's larger-than-life figure moved in disintegrating light across the screen.

Soon they would be on to another screen test. She was the eleventh out of "God knows how many." She might need acting lessons, but her slender body had symmetry and a merciless energy. He could imagine her drinking hooch or smoking in unfamiliar alleys where bottles had been broken, trash overfilled the barrels, and old posters lay torn and trampled on the ground. She could kiss a man and then bite him, drawing blood. She was a vamp. And he could imagine her naked, thrown against an unmade bed. Maybe his.

He drank the rest of his bourbon, puffed on his cigar. She was the kind of girl that could go crazy with desire. He'd seen that before with that starlet, Sarah Caldwell. The one that every morning pinned up all her hair and then let it fall down around her face all day long in a messy way. She'd gone on a holiday in Latin America and fucked every man in sight. The studio had to send someone out there to find her and bring her back, just in time to do her next movie. She was too wild, but the audiences sure liked her, especially the men. Last thing he heard she had joined the Communist Party and would only fuck Reds now. But at least the studio didn't have to watch her or baby-sit her anymore.

"Hey," he said more loudly, this time to the faceless man behind the noisy machine. "This one has sex appeal. Play her again."

Leon missed his own empty, ordered apartment. He vaguely remembered it, utilitarian shelves, a neat, clean bed, phonograph, and a table to eat on with two matching chairs. He found himself spending more time at work, where all the dramas seemed manageable with pencils and paper, all the mistakes could be erased and redone. There were no heroes, bourgeoisie, Communists, or Bohemian artists. You were what the numbers made of you, a fraudulent or an honest person. It was simple, but people's habits often gave them away, for example, a donation to certain causes or the purchase of a ridiculously expensive pair of shoes. The numbers created lives, a widow left with a large fortune or a starving cellist who could play Bach precisely, yet neither knew how to handle their money. When Leon met his clients, he was invariably disappointed. They became his secretary's, Alma's, friends, not his, and they were people who worked extra hours at the dime store or a small-boned, bald man dappled with freckles who owned a sawmill somewhere. Leon was retreating into his numbers, planning better lives for them.

"This drink smells like turpentine," Lil, her hair uncombed, some torn, ragged old clothes hanging from her shoulders, complained in her kitchen. The kitchen had dirty plates and pans scattered on the countertops, and garbage, potato peels, eggshells, dried tea, old napkins, and carrots gathered on the floor.

How could she tell what it smelled like?

"Remember when you lost an earring? It was the night you rubbed me with olive oil." He was reminiscing. He moved a wrinkled raincoat and wadded stockings so he could sit on her sofa. Her apartment had been dirty before, but he had never seen it quite so disorganized. A deep blue taffeta dress lay on the floor near the bedroom as though someone had just stepped out of it and carefully arranged it for viewing. It was just missing the body that belonged in it. Conversely, several hats lay rolled into a giant ball underneath her coffee table. The effect was that of a millinery shop that had exploded. But it also smelled. Food was dried in lumps on the table and in the corners of her room. Some of it was Chinese food with its distinct odor of ginger, oil, and garlic. She didn't want anything cleaned or moved. She wouldn't be able to find her way around.

"Ah," she said. "I have my own brand of art." She searched for something in the kitchen but couldn't remember what. "What happens next besides the obvious?"

Leon was silent. He didn't know how to answer her questions, which didn't make any sense. He could hear her rummaging through cabinets in the kitchen, tossing dinnerware aside, dropping things and then not picking them up.

"You want a wife, don't you?" Lil asked. But she had to pause and watch the leaping horses, which made lovely arcs against her kitchen wall. One was a luminous white with black spots and the other dark gray with white markings.

Their manes tossed into the air. Lil could see the panic in their eyes. When she walked through them she became half horse. She wondered if she could gallop.

Leon couldn't tell what would hold, what would dissolve. He could see Lil unraveling before him, like one of Alice's sweaters, and he didn't know what to do. "Come sit here," he patted the sofa in the living room, gently placed a torn book and a crusty fork on the floor.

Leon was an interruption, she thought, with his clean, lion-like hair and his predictable features. She was busy. What more did he want from her now? She had given him what she could, which might not have been enough, and yet she was fond of him. Perhaps in one of her other lives, she could have loved him almost as much as George. Lil sat down next to him. He stroked her hair and kissed her. She kissed him with her eyes open and fixed on him. She was grateful. He was here, she was fairly certain since she couldn't walk through him, along with her new cat, Chaos, appearing from under a chair. The cat reeled in the sunlight, her dark spots shivered as she lingered in the corner. She lunged at an imaginary ball. Lil knew that the cat wasn't real because she hadn't gone out and retrieved a cat, as far as she remembered, and she hadn't let one in. But Chaos came back again and again, and was a distraction. Everything felt nervous and frenzied, as in her dreams, which had happened so long ago.

Leon could hear her breathing. He touched her soft upper arm above her elbow. He felt the knot of her bones, the place where she had pinned her blouse closed instead of buttoning it. Her unruly hair spilled from her head, unbrushed. He would have unhappily shared her with George (until he left in his houseboat) but he couldn't share her with something he couldn't see or hear. It was a migratory pattern, to lose her, then gain her back again. As if he could really have her. Maybe it was something that she was compelled to reenact because of a deep need. The stillness of something broken rested between them.

"Let me give you a bath," he said gently.

He left her on the sofa, staring into a corner, as he scrubbed her claw-footed bathtub. In it he found a glass shattered into two pieces, a golf ball, a nail file, a page from a book that showed a woman's uterus and tubes climbing through her body, food splattered on one side like an abstract painting. He cleaned the tub quickly and ran the water. He returned to the other room, smiled at her as though she were a child. He couldn't send her to one of those places for insane people. "Think of Renoir's and Matisse's nudes. They're all pink, healthy, and clean."

"Yes," she said mechanically. "There are hazards from so much paint and from living in New York where there are too many people." But she couldn't take her eyes away from Chaos, who clawed at some invisible insect on her wall. The cat was batting at nothing, full of life and yet dissolving back into light, leaving wild, empty air. Lil traced the space where Chaos had played with her fingers. Then Lil obediently went into the noisy bathroom with its rushing water. She looked down at the water hurrying to fill the tub, with Leon standing there. She stared at the orbit of it, pulling her closer, wanting to pull her in. "I'll take a bath if afterwards you'll leave and not come back until I've called you to come over again."

"Okay," he agreed, noticing scratches along her ribs, a strip of swollen flesh near her pelvis as she slowly removed her clothes, her eyes staring and mesmerized by the water. Bruises trellised her spine and hipbone. Had she fallen or bumped into things? He momentarily regretted his acquiescence. He wanted to do more for her but she wouldn't have let him. He could only do as much as she would allow. When she sank into the warm water, her naked body looked so small and thin and helpless, almost a child's body. He started to soap her. Her damp hair clung to her cheeks and forehead, colorful stains began to disappear from her arms and legs, a kneecap and toes nudged the surface. He could feel her hipbones and the corrugated curves of her ribs through the washcloth. He bent down closer and could hear her low singing, but not the words. The blue veins that threaded her body were too visible in her upturned wrist. Her tiny, knotty scars. He wetted the branches of bone in her feet and worked his way up the trunks of her legs, toward her pelvis.

"Did I tell you about the woman who loved bathtub gin and drowned in it without getting to drink any of it? That great metaphor for life?" she asked. He nodded and continued his ablutions on her body.

She felt pinioned by water and tired of his attention. A tune kept returning inside her head that she had to hum or sing. Her body grew heavy, waterlogged, pulling her down. She didn't like dwelling on her body's details, the swollen toe or the chipped fingernail, a rib that ached when she breathed. She must have fallen down sometime and yet she couldn't remember it. She hated Leon for reminding her of all her faults and frailties, which became apparent in the clear water, and because he understood reality. When she was annoyed enough, she said, "That's enough. I can do this myself."

"Please just a little while longer." He thought about holding her under. That way she'd never lose her dignity, and he didn't know what else to do for her, really. He could ask Izzy or maybe Alice if they had any ideas. He didn't. Sometimes she seemed lucid, to clearly know her wants. He couldn't predict when she would be fine and when she wasn't even there with him. His washcloth returned to the places he knew by heart. He wanted to make her unhesitatingly clean. He wanted to linger with her body as long as he could until her mind returned. He hoped that after the gallery show she might improve. If only her body could speak, he thought, it was a fugitive map of her mind.

"I do love you in my own strange way. But I can't stay with you. Please go now."

Leon left, looking back at her once, her face still luminous and beautiful, wondering how much of her remained. She heard the front door close. She clenched her hands into fists. Then she relaxed, looked at her pale limbs and the floating washcloth. She thought: there is no humiliation in death. Her torso rose and she rubbed it with soap. She could hear everything and nothing. That song returned. She heard a man sobbing in her bathroom. When she looked up, she saw George all sugary with light, crying against the wall. She rose from the bathtub and dried herself with a towel. Her arm muscles ached as she reached toward him. She

could feel water cascading from her skin. She was suddenly
and without thought back in her clothes. She tried to hug
George, but he spilled from her hands, laughing now. He
paced her wall, searching for an escape. She couldn't help
him without destroying herself, her mind. She loved him
and, whispering, told him so. His clothes of light covered
her own body. She wanted him with her. She wanted him
within her. She wanted to feel his arms, the tickling of his
mustache. Instead, he was cleaved to her bathroom wall.
She kissed the wall's slick texture again and again. Her cat
appeared suddenly and the two moving pictures became
one. The cat rubbed George's legs and he kneeled to pet it.

"Come to me," she begged them. Lil wanted to join in,
but they ignored her. She retreated to the edge of her bathtub as she watched the washes of light and shadow, another faraway, untouchable world, the swimming of dusk and
illumination. Her new geography, new drama. Her whole
life was black and white, a moving painting that was visible only to her. She watched as George's ghost played with
Chaos.

She wondered briefly if she only wanted whatever she
couldn't have.

Dr. Duncan tapped his pencil repeatedly on his desk as he
acknowledged that his new client reminded him of Lillian
Moore. Lil was one of his few failures. Lil had left him a
telephone message that she wouldn't return to psychoanalysis, but she didn't say why. His white linen suit overlaid a
fuchsia-colored shirt, punctuated by his dark tie. He must

try another suit, he thought, in recognition of Lil. His clos-
est diagnosis of her was that she was neurotic, bordering
on schizophrenic, with psychotic tendencies exacerbated by
insomnia, but the analysis would have needed more time,
as would have the discovery of the causes and the attempt
at a cure. It was a shame that she had quit since they had
just barely scraped the surface of her childhood and attendant traumas and he suspected there was much more to discuss. But he wouldn't try to convince her to come back. That
would never work.

Before him the seventeen-year-old girl lay on the long,
gray, velvet couch surrounded by ivy. Her blonde hair
flowed over the surface of the couch. Dr. Duncan briefly
wondered how the spirit shaped the body. He wondered
whether it was forgetfulness or a deliberate action for this
girl to grow her hair so long. Details that added up to a phi-
losophy, to a way of living that foretold a life.

"I just couldn't help it. I liked to go up there alone, to the
roof of my family's building, and watch the sun go down. It
was the only time I liked, away from everyone. Everything
looked so tiny and far away." She stared at the ceiling, life-
less and inanimate in her explanation.

Dr. Duncan noticed the words "far away" and marked
it down. "So you wanted to show your little sister something?" She needed to talk about it, the accident.

"I was watching the sun, and my sister wanted to see it
too, but maybe I hoped that she'd find God for me instead."
She turned her head toward the window, to see the miniature broken body on the sidewalk again, the three-year-old
legs at awkward angles. Her sister had been impaled by a

metal fence before she hit the ground. She had watched it all in slow motion.

"Did she find God?" At least this girl didn't smell of cigarette smoke.

"Maybe she just pestered me too much and I pushed her." She knew there was no easy answer. "Maybe I loved her so much I wanted to keep her forever. Maybe she just fell, for no reason. I don't remember." She didn't move when Dr. Duncan's pencil hit the floor hard and bounced toward her. She didn't know whether she liked him or not.

He wrote down her reaction to the fall of the pencil. He fiddled with his tie. He noted that she made him nervous.

~

The Roving Reporter
Every Day He Asks Three Random People a Question

The Question: What do you think of the new comic strip in the N.Y. Daily News called "Little Orphan Annie"?

Dan Cohen, manager – That's the one with the little orphan girl with red hair and big eyes and Daddy Warbucks as her new millionaire father? I think she's a very lucky girl.

Miss Florence Anderson, stenographer – "Gee whiskers" and "Leapin' Lizards!"

Alice Holman, painter – I want to take Little Orphan Annie home and keep her.

~

Lamplight poured onto a table, onto the sofa that held George's horizontal body. The sofa was bolted to the floor. It was night and stars peppered the houseboat's portholes, then dropped onto the floor faintly, like regret. The end of George's mustache tickled the sofa back and his arms cradled his head. He stared unintentionally at the darkness in the corner that even the cold, damp air didn't seem to penetrate. He was wearing two sweaters that still didn't keep him warm enough. He counted all the years between his age and Alice's, all twenty-two of them. They had been together for six of them. He felt old, wrinkled, whitened, and yet he still could be distracted by all kinds of arousals, art, love affairs, photography, sex, boats. He enjoyed Shi, she would take him in her wooden arms and carry him away from his life into a brand new one. He would be an American in a foreign country. But he left her upkeep and guidance in more knowledgeable hands.

No one remained in the tiny galley where dirty dishes and glasses were accumulating. A used fork clanged repeatedly against a plate; water lapped against the boat. George remembered Lil's hips churning against his, Mary Beach's red hair falling through his open fingers, and Sophie, the dancer, who cried out loudly, like a singer in unequivocal pleasure.

He thought of the art in his exhibit lined up, in place, just waiting for his say-so. Afterwards, when the exhibit was over, everything dismantled or sold, a man would come and barge Shi away. He said he would tug their houseboat from Long Island to wherever they wanted to go, preferably along the East coast. George hadn't decided where to go yet. Somewhere he couldn't be found. Or else they would have to buy another boat, a sailboat, that could take them further away, to Europe or someplace warm. The man with the tug was named Kenneth and he was recommended by the man in the last berth, the bootlegger who kept his boat in the marina. George was afraid to trust anyone these days. Kenneth didn't want too much money, would leave them at their destination and go about his own business. George didn't want to know any more. Since Alice was becoming a sensation, George could sell Alice's paintings no matter where the two of them went.

The sensation came to the door and held the doorframe tightly because of the reverberations from another boat's extended wake. Her torn sweater had drips of green and black paint near the sleeves. The waves subsided and she released the frame. She looked out the window. "Watching stars floating on the ocean makes me want to try to paint the transitory water."

"Why not?" He scratched his mustache. "Maybe it's time to try painting something different. A maritime landscape."

"Maybe I should try to paint with someone else's eyes, some Egyptian type art." She sat on a chair. "Maybe I'm just thinking about that Egyptian show we saw at the Metropolitan Museum or the exotic Egyptian dancers we saw onstage in New York."

George laughed, thinking of their rigid, forced movements. "Everything Egyptian is so popular right now." He stopped. "That's it," he said suddenly.

"What?"

"We could go to Egypt the day after tomorrow." A sly smile emerged. "Egypt, Maine or Cairo, Massachusetts or, eventually, the real thing."

Alice looked at him. She shook her head slowly at the creaky wooden floor while the moon rose outside. "I'd miss New York." She sighed. She loved George's familiar, mischievous face and would forgive him almost anything. He could inspire new art movements, maybe even her own. "It's fine. Maybe I'll start a new painting now. The new place could knock me out of my old habits." She thought of George's recent behavior. "Maybe I'll start painting spoons and knives, dishes and crockery. The implements that transform fruit." She smiled. It wasn't about what you painted, but how you painted it, the style, the strokes, the vision. It would be something definitive, yet inexplicable.

Alice gathered up her painter's box and some blank canvases. A frown appeared, deepening the lines above her eyebrows. "First I must do a quick sketch of the water, before it changes." She moved into the next room mumbling, "It's trying to tell me something."

"Call me if you need any help," George yelled from the sofa.

"I will." A paintbrush fell from her arms and slapped the floor. "If I need you, I will." She scooped it back up and began.

When Alice was working on her art she was in her own world, surrounded by fruit, shapes and colors, paint, shadows or light, highlighted by foreshortening or perspective. She worked in a dream time where minutes felt suspended, and then they disappeared. Every bit of space in the room was studded with objects to paint. Alice needed to discover her own particular obsessions, allow them to possess her until she was done with them. George had walked into her studio a few times, waved to her, offered her coffee, and even brought her lunch once, but she didn't see him. To her, he wasn't really there unless he ruined her light.

George contemplated the blue flower pattern on a bowl set upon a table in the moonlight. He decided to tell Kenneth to come at two o'clock in the morning after the gallery show closed and take them toward Nova Scotia. He could go south too. He wouldn't tell him the precise destination, so no one would know where they planned to go, but he would leave him instructions in a sealed envelope on the boat for that night. Since Alice was indecisive in this way, he had to be certain that they left quickly enough. No questions asked. He needed to make sure they were safe from the men who carried guns hidden in their pockets and who wore buttons carved from human teeth. Once Mr. Beach had shown George a gold belt buckle he said was made of the fillings from his debtor's teeth. At first George didn't believe him and then, soon after, he did. The money he owed them was due in full the day after the gallery show ended, when he was supposed to have collected all the money due to him. George would run quickly, and go somewhere he hoped they wouldn't find him and Alice. He alone would know where they were going. Alice's paintings could provide them both with a good life.

Alice's eyes rushed to and from the window, trying to capture the patterns of the stars on the water. She used char-

coal on thick watercolor paper, completing it quickly. Then
she wanted to begin a painting, something unassumable
and new. Grapes arranged into planets, a cut apple as the
elongated face of the moon. Her room could be the heav-
ens. She was practicing her own kind of landscape until
she went somewhere different, to a place she couldn't yet
imagine, with twisted red plateaus and cliffs, or someplace
without clouds where the scanty trees doubled as umbrel-
las. Birds were confused by the light there. This was what
sand did: reformed our notions of shape; unrooted everything it touched; expressed itself unwillingly; inflicted itself
on every passerby; reduced all noise to a whisper. Art was
the part of Alice that was intangible and unshattered. She
would succumb to it, always. No questions asked. It was
who she was. She dappled some white onto orange, assem-
bled black into stray marks like rain. She had given up on
trying to know George because he moved farther away from
her in all the kind, little things he did for her. He became polite to her and more unapproachable, as if through etiquette
and ritual he would become blameless. She knew about Lil
and the dancer and she guessed at others, the married, red-
headed helper with her sweet daughter at the gallery. She
wanted to discuss them. But the fear of being forgotten and
the reproach to George kept her from saying anything. He
never did seem to want to talk about them, as if the nature of
their secrecy made the women seem more delicious to him.
So she was left with her art, the world reduced to seeing, her
imagination filling up a canvas. She was content. She would
always have what she carried around with her, what was
held in her overworked heart.

George tenderly kissed Alice's cheek. Her hand was moving rapidly across the canvas. She had already forgotten her own body. She didn't notice him, she was so engrossed in her painting. This was her world. To her George was invisible. She didn't feel anything, not even the gentle rocking of the houseboat.

Lil wanted color in her private moving pictures, a touch of azure, scarlet, chartreuse, saffron. She was tiring of black and white, the gray increments. She had even sworn off smoking cigarettes because the smoke compromised and veiled her wispy visions. But she still wasn't sleeping. She tried pinning some extra striped cloth on the wall when Chaos the cat appeared with a new sleek companion called Reality. Reality was licking its paws and Chaos rolled onto its back. But they just scampered across her cloth, they didn't seem startled by its presence, or include it in their romps. She wasn't even sure they had seen it. There was nothing she could do. She felt helpless in this other world. They reminded her of cats she had seen playing in an alley outside her building when she was a little girl. Sometimes she could talk to the moving pictures and they talked back and other times they were silent movies, which had little to do with her.

Lil was in her studio and she wanted to paint. She turned on her phonograph, playing Bach. She felt like a stone that the ocean had smoothed and washed over and over again. The cats faded, vanished. She could set up her paints and canvas, but she knew it was only a matter of time before more ghosts materialized. They wore her out. They were strange companions and difficult gifts that she would try to work around. Who would willingly want to receive them? She suspected what it would take to end them. A violin whined, too tinny. She would receive some money from George after the show, and the Beckers always supported much of the artwork that she did. It was too bad that she hadn't heard from the movie studio yet because her current world was make-believe. Acting would be easy. She would paint even if a magician or a cat or an old woman appeared. Maybe she would paint a dog to chase them all away. She was waiting for George.

Yellow felt buttery on her brush as she left a thick mark, her first, on the stretched, white canvas. It felt good. She wanted to slap paint onto the forbidding white expanse. Music reminded her of birds, their beaks and small bones uplifted in song. Or Izzy, her voice empty of anxiety or fear. Lil wasn't losing her mind, there was just too much of it. Lil turned too quickly and yellow drops spilled onto her painting. She liked the effect, would work it in. She had almost forgotten that it was winter outside, that all the lively speakeasies called her name.

The tulips that Leon had given her had died from neglect, their drooping symmetry stiff and dry. She wished it had been George that had sent them. She glanced out a window at the befuddled stars and the dank, dark night. How did she end up this way? Without George, without her child, talking to specters, a countless number of them following her, refusing to let her go. They were more manageable when they were quiet. They passed through her body sometimes, ignoring it, because they, too, didn't want to remain inside of her. She was growing accustomed to them. With them she didn't think about her future.

A dried yellow tulip petal fell onto the floor, where it curved like a thin smile. Music arrested her at a crescendo. She wondered if it was real. She had to question everything. She kicked a chair to see if it existed and her toes hurt through her slippers. Good, she thought, that must be a good sign. The sky could fall and she would have to test that also.

Day dawned and sunlight crawled slowly over the tops of buildings. Lil respected Leon's way with numbers, the defined spaces and shapes. They were concrete. The world lived inside of them. They were conclusive and obeyed the laws of cause and effect, supply and demand, and general measurement. Leon could make them dance and cry. She admired his abilities but she didn't need them. She wanted that bird that lived inside of her to peck or fly, the one that could split her in two just by fluttering or spreading its wings too far, the one that listened to instinct. Lil knew she should take another bath, but it seemed overwhelming. She wondered whose apples had sprouted in her still life. Maybe Alice had come. Some days it was hard to tell who had actually been there. Had Leon been there and had she sent him away? She wished Horace, her baby, would return. Lil didn't feel badly for Alice, she was becoming successful and could live in the mountains by herself and hardly notice that she was alone.

Lil's new, black telephone, the one the movie agent said she needed, made a mechanical sound that filled her room. She moved closer to it, in the living room, and stared at it until it stopped. She hoped it would crack open and disappear. She'd had too many calls from salesmen. That telephone was so demanding. Her curtains were hollow, full of air. The window was cold. Her body moved through transparent air to the kitchen where two remaining dishes crashed to the floor with insistent voices. It was funny how her mood could change. A cat jumped down from a bookcase, but she wasn't sure whether it was Chaos or Reality. Time and space are important, she thought. The cheap tulips were gone, had fallen away, lost their color and any scent they had originally had. Snow was predicted in the weather forecast. Lil liked the way snow plunged, covered, grew soft, and tried again. It didn't care what was already there, eclipsing everything. The hair that had fallen into her face seemed to be someone else's. She grazed the mahogany table with her finger. Her eyes ached and she rubbed them. Morning light touched her furniture gingerly. Lil walked back to her studio and looked at her painting. It was ugly and misshapen, with no sense of line or space. She threw it, wet, splattering onto the newspapers that hid her floor.

~

The Roving Reporter
Lil Asks Two Random People and
Two Cats a Question

The Question : What is in the future for George Holman and Lillian Moore?

The magician, name unknown—She will unravel and

discover tiny boxes full of anticipation. There's a restless-
ness called art that leaves her unrepentant. Will he pull
love from his sleeve and throw it away?
    Horace, the baby—The future remains uncertain.
    The cats, Chaos and Reality—Everyone is always wait-
ing until they finally pounce.

~

At the gallery's opening night Leon gazed at Lil's portrait
of Mary Beach, her red hair, her lips that looked overkissed,
a white scar along her leg that disappeared underneath her
white dress. A sensual portrait with winding flower stems in
the background and Mary swallowed by the bruise-colored
room and its collection of objects. Leon wanted to touch her
pulsing arteries, her translucent skin, even the bright, round
orange with Mary's fingers nearly grasping it. Numbers and
paint don't break down, he thought, at least for a long, long
time. They last longer than we do. They can express damage without being damaged themselves. Too bad he and Lil
couldn't last as long as her painting. He wanted to protect
her from bad weather, brush her hair, find a house where
they both could live. It was too hard and complicated. He
looked at the frame around Mary and knew that Lil lacked
borders.
    Leon wondered if Mary Beach would come to George's
Women's Exhibition or if Mr. Beach would even allow her
to go. The gallery was completely filled with people. But he
had not talked to anyone there yet or recognized someone
he knew. He inched closer to Mrs. Becker, who wore a me-

andering white fur draped over an expensive gown whose armholes dipped to her waist. Her flat chest nudged the draped material, pearls were suspended from her powdered neck. Then she disappeared. Leon didn't see Mr. Becker at all. An older woman teetered on high heels, eyebrows as thin as wires, and she poked her head between people to peer at the prices propped next to the paintings.

When the woman haltingly walked away, Leon saw Lil's next painting, one of her earlier works, flowers that seemed to be coughing. They were contained in dark rectangles like postcards from faraway places flying randomly through a field, the sun overlooking the scene.

A man in formal attire stamped his wet boots beside Leon, nudging him down to Lil's last painting, a diminutive harbor. One boat was larger and closer to the viewer. It looked suspiciously like George's houseboat although Lil had painted it before George bought the boat. A tiny figure, small as a child, seemed to be on the boat, but Leon couldn't decipher who it was. Seagulls the size of coins circled in the sky. Leon decided that he couldn't help wanting the kind of relationship he wanted with Lil. It was just that, perhaps, she wasn't the right person to have it with. The past pulsed through everyone's lives, shaping them, especially Lil's past. He looked around, women's faces emerged, all ages, shapes, and sizes. They couldn't explain his failure to him. He concentrated on the tiny figure in Lil's piece until it resembled the number five, until the man next to him pushed Leon with his coat. If Leon could understand her painting, maybe he could understand her. He wasn't really interested in Alice's or anyone else's work. Then he heard Lil's husky voice behind him. When he turned, Lil appeared groomed and coherent, wearing a flapper dress, not dressed as a rag-a-muffin. She was talking to a short woman with gold-painted fingernails, crimped blonde hair and a folded umbrella that was dripping water across the floor. Leon was tracing the puddles she left.

"Mr. Drake took these dolled-up photographs of me, and I've sent them to all the moving picture studios," the woman said loudly. Her sequined dress beneath her thin coat murmured in agreement. She batted thick eyelashes as Leon approached. She touched Lil's arm, and as Lil pulled away, she dropped her hand. "You should try it for a little extra dough. You'd be great. You're a natural."

Lil found a cigarette in her beaded handbag, attached it to the holder, lit it, and blew smoke past the woman's face. "Yes, I might, Elsie." A distracting fly buzzed around Elsie's face, landing on her nose. But Lil wasn't sure. It flew to the top of Elsie's head and sat near the dark roots of her hair. There weren't any flies in winter, were there?

"Photographs were the original basis for movies. Thirty years ago the Magic Lantern projected glass slides one at a time for audiences. Then the photographer Muybridge recorded a horse running to study motion. He tried to prove that all four feet of the horse left the ground at specific points in time. Then there was Thomas Edison's Vitascope projector, along with George Eastman's invention of roll and transparency film, that began the moving pictures we see today," Leon said, running a hand through his blonde hair. The other hand held his hat at his side.

"That's just ducky, Mr...?" Elsie tilted her head. One eyebrow arched as though it had a life of its own.

"Mr. Shaffer. Please call me Leon." He shook her moist, warm hand.

"You look familiar, Leon." A slight frown appeared on her forehead, and a finger raised up to her lips. "Are you a friend of Lil's?"

Elsie and Leon both looked at Lil, who was staring intently at the top of Elsie's head, though neither knew why. Lil's smoke drifted to a sculpture, clothed the plaster figure there.

"Yes, I respect her work."

Conversations interrupted them, people pushing by, saying things like, "This one really has something going," or "You can never tell with dames," or "I heard that he threw her over for another one." Their space grew smaller. They huddled closer together. Lil barely had room to move.

Elsie swept her arm toward Leon but someone bumped it away. "I met Lil at a restaurant when we both reached for our coats on a rack at the same time." She laughed in high-pitched little shouts.

Lil could barely follow the conversation. People were getting too close to the paintings. She wanted to shoo them away. Throngs of people were there to see the exhibit of women artists. She couldn't bear to think of them poking at her work, making comments. She hadn't decided what to do about the obnoxious black fly flitting along the dark furrows of Elsie's hair. It challenged her to chase it away.

"What do you think of the show?" Leon asked Elsie politely.

"I haven't really seen it all yet." Elsie's toe dug into

George's floor. Her heavy, black eyelashes laboriously lifted to Leon. "I know where I saw you. It was in the newspapers. You were a reporter on the Leopold and Loeb case."

"No."

"Then, weren't you the one that stopped a robbery or saved a girl from drowning or messed up some flimflam men, or something?"

At that moment Lil finally swatted at the fly that had been rubbing its legs together greedily above Elsie's blonde crimped hair. It flew across the room and landed on George's shoulder where he was talking to an animated dark-haired woman. Lil felt her palm hit Elsie's head.

Elsie looked shocked. She said from below both raised eyebrows, "Well, I must go and take in the rest of the show now." She left, leaving small, wet splashes behind her.

Izzy almost slipped on one of Elsie's puddles but Marco grabbed her elbow. "It's snowing out there."

"We're enjoying the extraordinary art and the surrealistic crowds," Marco said, eyeing a man in a top hat with strings of garlic around his neck.

"Lil," Izzy called her. Lil's head swung toward Izzy. "Your paintings are songs with lovely titles."

"Thank you," Lil responded. But Izzy's lips and bones appeared to leap toward Lil. Lil watched a man's cigarette smoke dancing with smoke from other cigarettes, a waltz that rose toward the ceiling. She would keep that knowledge to herself and not say anything about all that coiling in the air. Lil didn't miss sleeping anymore. The world was full of things to see and do, private expeditions. Sometimes she felt rain falling in her mind, echoing. Everything grew complicated and tired her. All movement and thought was a struggle. She could live in her own world, one of painting and George, begin her own language, strange consonants and vowels, twisted and cracked open to reveal their interiors. A pictorial language.

Izzy looked around the gallery but couldn't see farther than the surrounding few people. She was searching for Alice, who was wandering around in a new purple sweater with sequins and a black skirt that hung down too low on one side. She looked sparkling and lopsided. People had been talking to Alice and she was shyly becoming undone. Marco had pulled Izzy aside and whispered to her, "Let's go find Alice and take her home to her boat. She's had enough of the party and wants to miss the Becker's usual reception. She's telling people she doesn't feel well." Izzy and Marco intertwined their arms. Marco said, "We'll be eating Chinese later if you want to join us," to Lil and Leon.

"Thank you," Leon replied. After they left he said to Lil, "It'll do Alice some good to get away." But Lil didn't respond to his hint. A woman with a tray was trying to offer appetizers all around, but they were scooped up immediately. She left quickly, crushed in a sea of people. The silver moon of her tray was turned onto its side and tucked under her arm.

"So is our relationship seasonal?" Lil said hurriedly to Leon, having spotted George talking to a couple who resembled black cats in their dark clothes. She began to walk through the masses of people and Leon followed her. She stopped to light a cigarette, which was usually forbidden in the gallery, with a silver lighter the man in the top hat offered her. She slipped the lighter into her handbag and moved on. The man was pushed in another direction by masses of people. He didn't seem to care. She was one of the women artists, after all.

"It's forever," Leon yelled, rushing to keep up with her.

"Nothing lasts forever. And you know about George."

Leon could see her in front of him, moving too fast. Her harsh voice, her beaded dress shaking, her dark bob, her receding figure. People moved in and out between them. His heart screamed, unnerving him. He gulped air. He tried to follow her smoke but it flew away and mingled with other smoke. He saw her back growing even smaller. "I know some things."

"That's enough," she shouted. "I'll see you later at the party." And she disappeared.

Baby Chapman took her place. "I remember you from another party." The cans strung around her neck had labels with women on them, buoyant women sitting on rocks above a sea full of fish, a fleshy woman mixing peas and onions in a bowl, a woman mashing cherries. Baby Chapman's graying hair was fluffed into curls. "I'm so joyful that this is a Women's Art Exhibit." Baby had two men in tow. One casually crossed his legs and lit up a cigarette. The other was taller, with a beard. He kept his eyes on Baby.

"Yes, hello, Baby Chapman." Leon was still confused and dismayed.

"I'll have to invite you to one of my parties soon." She left, swaying from side to side, and the men followed her. Her cans noisily drummed against one another, but Leon couldn't hear them because the sound was lost amid the chatter and laughing.

"This car was entrusted to me and to me alone by Mrs. Becker," Lil told George from behind the wheel of the Beckers' Packard Runabout Roadster. "The Beckers wanted to ride with someone else." The automobile had white tires with spokes and the exterior shone black and hard as a carapace. The white convertible top rattled just above their heads. Lil's gloved hands gripped the wheel, pushing George's hand away when he asked her if he could drive it. Leon sat in the rumble seat in the back. He couldn't hear anything.

They had been among the few stragglers left at the gallery. Everyone else had left for the Beckers' country house and Lil had declined to go with anyone who offered. She had wanted to stay to the very end. Leon and George also stayed. Alice, Marco, and Izzy were gone already. She had offered George a ride to the Beckers' and he had accepted. She was delighted. Then Leon had insisted that he go along with them, needing a ride. He said he would be fine in the rumble seat when she told him there were only two seats in the front of the Roadster and that she and George needed them.

Darkness cradled them as they glimpsed of trees and houses along the periphery, which were barely lit by their headlights. It was the end of the world. She didn't need to tell George anything. He knew it all and he had always known. Snow concealed everything along the road. They quickly passed objects she could no longer recognize. The car hovered along the edges villainously.

More snow began to fall. Lil thought of Beck Salsbury slashing one of her paintings at the show with a cheese knife before she'd allow a woman she didn't like to buy it. The painting, with a cowboy hat and a horse, was hanging in shreds. It sat tucked in the trunk, along with two of Marguerite Zorach's portraits that hadn't sold. Lil was glad that she hadn't attacked one of her own works, as people would have taken that as further proof of her losing her mind. Although who could tell the difference these days? More rumors would have flourished.

"I sold all the paintings, including all of yours, except for what's in this car," George stated. "It was my best show." He pulled on his mustache as the canopy over their heads grew heavy and wet with snow.

"Who bought my portrait of Mary?" It was difficult talking above the noise of the engine.

"The Beckers."

"Then where would you like to go, George? You know that we don't have to go to the Beckers' house." They were already half way there and Lil was driving too fast through the snow. The lights of New York City had dimmed at least an hour ago. Every dark thing around them whitened from their headlights. Lil could see the general outline of bare branches that had been indistinguishable in the night.

"Heigh ho, it's off to the Beckers' we go." George stuck his hand out the car window and felt the snowy wetness on his palm. He had sipped from someone's flask at the party, but not too much. "What about Leon in the back?"

"We could drop him off somewhere, near the Beckers' if he wanted. No, seriously, George. I can keep driving and we could go anywhere you want, anywhere in the world. You could send for your boat or leave it for Alice." She was begging.

George didn't want to agitate Lil. He slipped further down into his leather seat. He could feel it accommodating his body. "I want to go to the Beckers'." Poor Leon, with the wind and all that snow in the back. George thought of Alice's cheekbones, her fine hair. He had chosen her. "I'm just another entertainment for you besides art. I'm a diversion. And that's all I can be."

"I'm becoming immune to art. It doesn't matter to me. I don't feel it anymore," she said in a strange voice. The car passed a house near the side of the road where she believed she saw an old woman in her nightgown twirling near a gate, her arms akimbo, her mouth open and catching snow. When Lil glanced back in the mirror, a child's snowman, with branches for arms, sat comfortably in the yard. "Do you think marriage changes anything? Did it earn you any forgiveness?"

"Not from you, maybe from Alice."

"Why? What did you do to Alice?"

"It's more about what I didn't do for her."

Too many objects in the night lacked borders. The snow merely highlighted their blurriness. Lil felt air pushing the car. In the rush of it were all the individual snowflakes, each one different. She could feel the beads of her dress pressed between her skin and the car seat. Her dark bob flew excitedly around her face. She could feel one party shoe pressed against the gas pedal. She put a hand outside her window and the flakes were as soft as paintbrush bristles. A glitter-

ing, borrowed necklace clustered at her throat. She wanted
to ask if she could borrow George from Alice for a while
since he was all she had left. George would answer that she
enjoyed the idea of him – a Cubist George caught in many
positions or a Modern George using rudimentary brushstrokes to suggest himself. Instead she said, "I always wanted to make something monumental, something beautiful
that could walk on its own."

"Art," George nodded complicitly. "One for the road."
But his words were lost in the sudden roaring of the engine.

Lil saw something dark and crying in the snow in front
of the car before the car turned, almost by itself, and broke
through a short fence. Was it the baby again? She didn't feel
any surprise or urgency as the car leaped, bumping over
rocks and bushes, and then plunged into lake water. They
were too far into the middle of the familiar lake, the one on
the Beckers' property, the one where Leon had rescued that
frightened woman and had briefly been famous. Small, cold
waves pushed the car, then pulled its dark, halted body,
folding over the black front and sides.

For a moment their eyes met. She remembered that
George couldn't swim either. She glanced at the back of the
car but Leon was gone. He wasn't imprisoned by the car
canopy. He could swim. But he wasn't near them, rescuing
them. She was glad. She wanted Leon saved, would have
tried to push him out herself. It was always her and George.
Had Leon even been there?

She peered into the lights winking from tents at the Beckers' party. She hoped that no one had heard or seen them.
She could feel snow in her hair, the cold water lapping at

her legs. A tug, like a current, embraced her, a pulse in her heart. She was happy. She took George's cold hand in hers. The water would swallow them soon.

George pulled his hand away and frantically tried to undo the doors and canopy, calling for help, "Leon, Leon, where are you? Is anyone out there?" His gray mustache grew dark and soggy. George was submerging quickly.

The party had just begun, and since it was snowing, no one was out near the lake. Water rushed in. They were sinking fast. George's eyes were wide with fear and shock. Lil closed her eyes but they sprung open. She tried to take his hand again but he pulled it away.

"This is much bigger than the bathtub full of gin," she said, but George hadn't heard her. There was a faint strain of voices and music in the distance. She wasn't certain whether she was in a car or not.

At that moment:

Leon was still sprawled on the snowy ground at the Beckers' where he had hit his head on a rock.

Herbert, the lion, howled from inside a room.

The Beckers were dancing a tango together in the main tent at their party.

Dr. Duncan tapped his pencil on a table at home, thinking about his new, young patient.

Izzy and Marco sat alone at a large table in the Chinese restaurant, waiting for the others to come.

Alice began a new painting on the houseboat that would dock at the secret place George had chosen. She wondered if George was going to arrive later, or whether he had met someone new and wasn't coming at all.

Lil's mother beckoned to her.

The baby, Horace, held out its arms.

The telephone at Lil's apartment was ringing with a call from the motion picture studio.

Was George strolling with Mary Beach along the shore of the lake? Mary was holding Beatrice's tiny hand and Beatrice was skipping.

Several unknown artists were in a speakeasy, ordering more drinks and toasting to "A future very different from the past." Just as they had done last night and the night before.

The morning headlines blared:

Two Artists Dead While Hero and Accident Victim, Leon Shaffer, Recovering

There was a photograph of Leon with a bandaged head onthe front page. Along with the Leopold and Loeb case.

Later Leon would find himself describing Lil as "the one who got away," at dinner parties in order to explain why he never married. He bought the portrait of Mary Beach from the Beckers. Eventually he stopped talking about Lil altogether.

Laurie Blauner is the author of two other novels, *Somebody* and *Infinite Kindness*. The books received a King County Arts Commission and a 4Culture award, respectively. She is also the author of a novella and six books of poetry. She has received grants for her writing from the National Endowment for the Arts and Artist Trust. Her poetry and fiction have appeared in *The New Republic, The Nation, The Georgia Review, Poetry, American Poetry Review, Mississippi Review, (Short) Fiction Collective, Subtle Fiction,* and many other journals and magazines. She lives in Seattle, Washington. Her web site is www.laurieblauner.com.